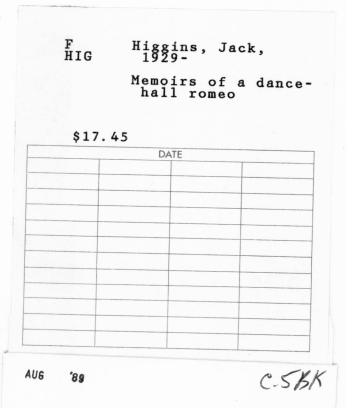

F
HIG

Higgins, Jack,
1929-

Memoirs of a dance-
hall romeo

$17.45

DATE			

AUG   '89

C-5BK

JACK HIGGINS

SIMON AND SCHUSTER

MEMOIRS OF A DANCE-HALL ROMEO

A NOVEL

New York London Toronto Sydney Tokyo

Simon and Schuster
Simon & Schuster Building
Rockefeller Center
1230 Avenue of the Americas
New York, New York 10020

Designed by Deirdre C. Amthor

Manufactured in the United States of America

10   9   8   7   6   5   4   3   2   1

Library of Congress Cataloging-in-Publication Data
Higgins, Jack.
    Memoirs of a dance-hall romeo.

    I. Title.
PR6058.I343M46   1989   823'.914   89-11299
ISBN 0-671-67843-4

In grateful remembrance of all the girls of those far-off days, but especially the ones who said yes. . . .

Of all sexual aberrations, perhaps the most peculiar is chastity.

—Remy de Gourmont

Dancing is a wonderful training for girls. It's the first way you learn to guess what a man is going to do before he does it.

—Christopher Morley

1 AVA

*Men who do not make advances to women are apt to
become victims of women who make advances to them.*
                                        —Walter Bagehot

... and so, I decided to devote myself exclusively to
the pursuit of women. For a callow youth of twenty,
a momentous decision, breathtaking in its impu-
dence. It took so many things for granted. Not least,
that the necessary women would make themselves
available.

It's almost impossible to say where anything be-
gins or ends, but Ava, I suspect, would be as good a
starting point as any. I never knew her last name.

11

She was just a girl who picked me up on the top deck of a bus in the early autumn of 1949.

It was the second day of my demobilization leave and I had returned home, not from war, but from the army, an important distinction for one who had run to the recruiting office two years earlier, happy to be conscripted, a refugee from an insurance office. Hungry for adventure, I joined the Intelligence Corps and volunteered for field security work in Palestine, where there was some sort of shooting war going on.

I arrived in time to spend exactly one month in a transit camp in Jaffa before coming home again along with everyone else as the tide of empire started to turn. After that little episode, the War Office posted me to Berlin, probably because I couldn't speak German, and I spent the rest of my service working in an office nine till five, processing personnel records with the acting rank of sergeant (paid) to help my meager authority.

Suddenly it was all over and I was home again. The same and yet not the same. Desperately wanting everything to have changed and finding that nothing was different. Home to Manningham, the pride of the West Riding, to the Victorian town hall, rattling trams, cobbled streets. A cloth-cap society which hadn't changed much since the thirties.

Six weeks' leave and I'd have to go back to work, and it would be as if nothing had happened in between at all. I thought of the Incorporated Insurance Society and my old chair waiting for me by the third-story window no more than two dozen times a day, and the memory rose like bile to choke me.

Which brings me to Ava, for on the second night,

fleeing from the depression which had seized me at the very thought of being back home for good, I took a bus out to a village pub four or five miles from Manningham. It was a place I had frequented during that last year before joining the army. There wasn't a soul I knew. I spent a wretched couple of hours standing at the bar, drank three pints of light ale and two whiskeys, then left and stood at the bus stop on the main road.

A thin rain was falling, which didn't particularly bother me as I had my greatcoat over my shoulder. I pulled it on and waited another five minutes or so until the bus came; I was morose, bitter, and rather enjoying the melancholy drama of it all.

When the bus came, I paid the guard on the platform and went straight up to the top deck. Around a dozen girls were squeezed together into the three rear seats, all chattering loudly. The voices ceased as I appeared, the uniform, I suppose. They were tarts to the last man, what my Aunt Alice would have called dead common, the head scarves, short skirts, and platform heels like a uniform.

One of them said, "Isn't he lovely?"

There was a general laugh, and I moved on hurriedly to sit in an empty seat across the aisle from two middle-aged couples. A naval shore station at Haxby three or four miles back along the road trained sick-berth attendants and clerks—the girls would have been to some dance or other there, I supposed. I glanced over my shoulder. They had their heads together, whispering busily, looking toward me at the same time.

Another called, "Hello, handsome," and I turned away and lit a cigarette.

I had never been much good around girls. One or two abortively messy episodes and an overheated imagination had kept me going before the army. Service in Berlin during the airlift had offered a promise of untold delights. A city of sin where a woman could be had for five cigarettes. As the official Naafi canteen ration was one hundred and twenty-five a week at the time, the prospect had seemed limitless.

I had indulged once, with a blond lady old enough to be my mother, in a back room at a cellar club—an affair noted more for its extreme briefness than for anything else. Some days later I had entered the washroom at the barracks in time to see the lad who had accompanied me on this adventure, an old Harrovian no less, emerge from the lavatory with a cry of agony, clutching his private parts. He disappeared in the general direction of the medical room where a certain unfortunate social disease was diagnosed without too much trouble.

It was enough. I withdrew from the fleshpots and enrolled in a correspondence course for an external degree from the University of London. Not much of a substitute for a boy already three years past his sexual peak, according to the experts, but fear is a great persuader.

I stared out into the night, rain pattering against the window, and in its dark mirror a girl appeared and sat down beside me. "Got a fag to spare, Jack?" she asked.

I suppose she was about eighteen, although you could never be sure with girls like her. Frizzy ginger hair poked from beneath the head scarf and she was badly made up, the mouth a vivid orange smear. And the skirt was a couple of feet too short at a time when the new look was really taking hold and most girls wore their skirts well below the knee.

She was the kind of girl I'd usually have run a mile to get away from, but those two whiskeys on top of the light ale had nicely dulled my senses, and the breasts beneath the oyster satin blouse, where her cheap raincoat swung open, were round and firm, and the nipples sharply pointed.

In fact she suddenly looked about the most attractive thing on earth. I produced a tin of Benson and Hedges, marked "For His Majesty's Forces Only" and offered her one.

She held onto the tin and examined it greedily. "These look nice. The navy boys at Haxby only get Woodbines."

I gave her a light, she blew out smoke expertly and looked me over. "On leave, are you?"

I tried to sound the tough, devil-may-care soldier. "That's it, love."

One of the girls from the rear of the bus called, "Hey, Ava, what's he in? The Cadet Corps?"

Ava jumped up, turned and leaned so far over the back of the seat that the raincoat and short skirt lifted together, exposing a generous expanse of stocking top and the bottom half of her rear encased in the tightest pair of red pants I'd ever seen in my life.

"Why don't you get stuffed?" she called.

"Disgusting," one of the middle-aged ladies on the other side of the aisle muttered. "You ought to do something, Albert."

But Albert, as sad-looking a specimen of the British workingman as I have ever seen in his old tweed overcoat and cloth cap could only stare, mesmerized, at Ava's bottom, sweat on his brow, his hands tightly clenched in his lap.

The guard appeared briefly at the top of the stairs. "Any more of that and you're all off," he called sternly.

One of the girls stood up and put her arms around his neck and he retreated in confusion.

Ava sat down, crossed one leg over the other and rubbed it against my thigh. "Do you live in Manningham, Jack?" she demanded.

Her voice seemed to come from very far away and the light bulb above my head dimmed suddenly as the whiskey fumes rose into my brain.

I took a couple of deep breaths and forced myself to my feet. "You'll have to excuse me. I get off here."

I brushed past her, stumbled down the stairs and found myself on the platform, mysteriously still in one piece. There was a lot of laughter going on upstairs, but by then I had only one thing on my mind. Fresh air and plenty of it.

The bus slid into the curb and I dropped off, lurched across the pavement and grabbed at some garden railings to steady myself.

A familiar voice called, "Hey, Jack, wait for me."

I turned and saw Ava jump off the platform just as the bus pulled away. She stood beneath the streetlamp, legs slightly apart, hands pushed into the pockets of her raincoat, an accusing smile on her face.

"Trying to drop me, were you?"

God knows what had made her follow. Probably the jeers of her friends, although at that precise moment in time I was too miserable to care.

"I just don't feel so good, that's all."

She produced the tin of Benson and Hedges. "You forgot your cigs."

"You can keep them," I said. "I thought I told you that."

My stomach seemed to turn over and I staggered around the corner into a narrow alley and was thoroughly sick. Rainwater spouted from a broken fallpipe. I filled my cupped hands, rinsed my mouth and splashed some over my face, which made me feel considerably better although my head still seemed to belong to somebody else.

My chief recollection of the whole affair, and of subsequent events, is of a total lack of reality. The intense quiet, except for the rushing of the rain, the lights of the streetlamps flickering on the wet asphalt. I was adrift in a strange dreamlike world where things happened soundlessly and in slow motion as if under water.

Somehow Ava was very close now, pulling my hands inside her raincoat, leaning against me. "I know what you need, Jack," she murmured. "Just what the doctor ordered."

She kissed me greedily and at the same time unbuttoned my trousers with a speed and skill that argued long practice. It was enough to make Saint Anthony himself forget every good resolution he ever made, and I surfaced instantly and started to unfasten her blouse.

She shook her head and pulled away slightly. "Not here, Jack. I know just the place. Much better than this."

By then I was so thoroughly aroused that I would have followed her anywhere, and I went obediently, my hand in hers, across the road to the playing fields on the far side.

There was a hut over there used as a changing room by various sports clubs. The door banged to and fro in the slight breeze, the lock long since forced by vandals, and when we went inside, light from one of the streetlamps drifted in through the broken window.

She turned and reached for me, a hand inside my trousers again. When we kissed I noticed that she was trembling slightly, yet saw no particular significance in this. The simple fact was that I couldn't believe it was really happening.

"Come on, Jack," she said urgently. "Put your coat on the floor."

I did as I was told and she lay down in the patch of light from the window and pulled off her pants briskly.

I stood staring down at her, mesmerized, and there was a touch of impatience in her voice when she said, "Let's be having you then."

I sprawled across her, trembling like a leaf, pushed my hands inside the blouse, shoved up the bra and reached for those plump, sharply pointed breasts.

What happened then can still at a distance of some twenty years bring me out in a cold sweat, for they came away in my hands, so to speak. It was several seconds before I realized that I was clutching two largish balls of cotton wool, and the unpalatable fact remains that Ava was about as flat as it is possible to be.

She seemed completely oblivious to all this, her body trembling violently as she spread her legs. The moment I entered her, breasts or no breasts, I discharged.

It was a tremendous disappointment, the whole thing so instantly accomplished. I went slack and so did she, but only for a moment. She pushed me violently to one side and sat up.

"Thanks for nothing," she said.

She stood up and pulled on her pants. "Call yourself a man," she said, then slapped me solidly across the face, turned and marched into the night.

I stood in the small porch of the changing hut and watched her go, back in that unreal world again where nothing seemed to make much sense except some instinct for self-preservation that reminded me to button my trousers before walking sadly home through the rain.

• • •

When I was in the first form at grammar school, Jake O'Reilly was in the lower sixth and waiting to go into the forces, which meant that we were hardly bosom friends, in spite of the fact that he lived just around the corner in the same quiet backwater of Victorian houses next to Ladywood Park.

But all that had changed after my first leave. At loose ends one night, I attended a meeting of a local literary society and found Jake, who had just been demobilized. Over the coffee we discovered a mutual interest in writing.

He had produced a considerable number of short stories without selling a thing, and I had churned out three-quarters of a novel that could only be described as a parody of Hemingway at his worst.

Jake was a Yorkshire Irishman, a bad mixture, especially when he had been drinking, but there was little doubt that he was the wisest man I knew—very definitely what Aunt Alice, who was greatly interested in such matters as spiritualism and the occult, would have termed an "old soul."

When I reached home after the Ava disaster, I went around the corner to see if his light was on.

His house, like ours, had been built at the high tide of Victorian prosperity for affluent wool merchants and solicitors, with pointed Gothic towers at each corner and substantial outbuildings. His mother, who was a widow, had split the place into two large flats and several bed-sitters.

Jake himself had a sort of studio-bedroom over the garage at the rear, and the light was on. I went up the fire escape, leaned over the landing rail and peered inside. He was sitting at the desk by the window busily making notes from a book propped up before him, which was where I was to find him on most evenings during the year that followed, for he was trying to make up for the years lost to the navy by passing his Law Society examinations at one fell swoop.

I poked my head around the door. "Can I come in?"

He swung around in the chair. He is probably the most engagingly ugly man I have ever known in spite of the blue eyes and flaxen hair of an S.S. officer in a Hollywood movie. His nose had been broken in some fracas or other, for Jake had enjoyed what is known as a hard war, courtesy of the Royal Navy, as a member of the crew of a torpedo boat working the Channel out of Falmouth.

He examined me gravely. "You look terrible. Would you like a beer?"

"Never again," I said and made for the couch by the fire.

He didn't say a word—simply plugged in the electric kettle, went into the bathroom and came back with something fizzing merrily away in a glass of water. I got it down and he sprawled in the chair opposite and lit a cigarette.

"What happened to you?"

I told him about Ava in some detail. By the time I had finished, the kettle was steaming and he got up and made some tea.

"So what's your problem?" he demanded. "Most blokes I know would think they'd had a reasonably satisfactory night of it."

"Ava wouldn't," I said.

"All right, so you were a bit quick off the mark. Women like to experience the big bang too, you know."

I sat there sipping scalding tea, an expression, I suspect, of reasonably settled gloom on my face. Jake went into the bathroom. He returned with his face well lathered, and shaved in the mirror above the fire.

I was somewhat mystified by these proceedings but contented myself by saying, "It's all right for you."

"If it is, it's been a long, hard road. Did I ever tell you where I spent the morning of my eighteenth birthday? Drifting around the middle of the English Channel in a life jacket. We hit a mine on my third patrol."

"What happened?"

"Nothing very much. It was bloody cold. I thought I was going to die and I'd never have known what it was like to sleep with a woman. That thought circled endlessly in my brain."

"One of life's great experiences missed?"

"Exactly." He paused, wiping lather from his face. "I remember coming into Falmouth in the lifeboat, wrapped in blankets, with a crowd watching from the quay. It made me feel very satisfyingly like a veteran."

"And the other business?" I asked. "What about that?"

"Found myself a lady of the town that very night. Two quid down the drain." He smiled that slow, gentle, wry smile of his. "An experience to be noted for its brevity more than anything else, just like you and your Ava. But it changed me, I must confess."

"In what way?"

"I became convinced that I was going to die. Some sort of delayed anxiety reaction to being blown out of the sea."

I found it difficult to take the remark seriously, and I suppose it showed, for he held up his hand and added, "I used to lie awake at night waiting for my heart to stop, which seemed a significant waste of the time one spent in bed. You could say I turned to women in desperation."

"With success?"

"A uniform went over very well in those days." He took a dressing gown from behind the door and put it on. "Come to think of it, there wasn't much I turned down. Naafi girls, Wrens—anything in a skirt

22

in a dance hall, usually through a reasonably alcoholic haze."

"But what if you'd caught something?" I said. "Didn't that ever worry you?"

"But I thought I was going to die, don't you see?" he said patiently. "That was the whole point. Nothing seemed to matter very much. It's true what they say, you know. Nothing succeeds like excess. There was a terribly nice W.V.S. lady at one of the canteens who invited me round to her place for a bingo drive. Turned out she'd got the wrong night."

"What happened?"

"I stayed for tea." He smiled. "Opened up an entirely new field of operations. Then there was a young lieutenant in a certain paramilitary religious organization who gave me the most stimulating afternoon of my life in the rest room of a church hall in Plymouth after she'd closed the canteen."

I gazed at him in awe. "So what do you do now? You never go out. You're always at that damn desk studying."

"I can see you're missing the point entirely," he said. "Let's put it this way. Most men spend a large proportion of their time at the office desk or factory bench thinking loose thoughts about their neighbor's wife, or the girl behind the bar at the local, or what have you. But not me. I'm a free man. I can keep sex in its place because I worked through it. In other words, it doesn't run my life, it's just another part of it."

"Thanks to all those willing ladies in Falmouth and Plymouth during the war?"

"Exactly. No psychological hang-ups. No traumas. I even sleep nights."

"So what am I supposed to do?"

"Lay Ava's ghost, old sport. Try one of the local dance halls. Try all of them, come to that. Lots of girls available there. Every shape and size known to man and they're all lovely. Just remember every woman's beautiful in some way or other, and you can't go far wrong."

I stared at him, unable to think of any useful comment, and he sighed heavily.

"For God's sake, Oliver, if you don't get them out of your system now, you'll go through the rest of your life spending about ninety percent of your waking hours brooding over women and the flesh. As for your dreams, I shudder to think what they'll be like." He hauled me to my feet. "Now get to hell out of here and let me get on with some work. And keep me posted."

It was raining hard when I went down the fire escape. When I turned and looked up he was standing in the doorway, a curiously elegant picture in that silk dressing gown, his white-blond hair glinting in the light.

"Goodbye, old sport," he said.

This had become a ritual with us after seeing Alan Ladd in *The Great Gatsby* earlier that year, and through the film discovering the book.

"They're a rotten crowd," I shouted. "You're worth the whole damn bunch of them put together."

He raised his hand, Gatsby to the life, then went inside. I moved as far as the shrubbery and paused, thinking suddenly that he had gone to considerable pains with his appearance for the sake of a law book or two.

I was intrigued, and with good cause as it turned

out, for some minutes later the back door of the house opened and the tenant of one of the flats, a young war widow named Amy Tarrant, ran across the yard with a raincoat over her shoulders. Jake greeted her warmly on the landing and drew her inside.

I was surprised. Aunt Alice had told me that Mrs. Tarrant, with two young boys to support, had her sights set on a career rather than on a second husband; she was already deputy headmistress of a girls' secondary school at twenty-nine.

It was many years later when Jake let slip that for a time they had enjoyed a mutually satisfactory relationship, meeting two or three occasions in the week in the way I had witnessed.

I felt a strange sense of betrayal that night. I wanted to feel that in Jake I had found that most difficult of all things to find in this world—a friend in the deepest sense of the word. Someone with whom one could exchange confidences and bare the soul. Yet already there were secrets.

Still, his advice seemed sound enough. I gave it some thought on the way home, and later, a good deal more, sitting in the darkness by the turret window of my bedroom, smoking a cigarette, staring out at the rain.

God knows why, but it always seemed to be raining on those quiet nights so long ago. Great silver cobwebs of the stuff drifted through the gaslight beyond the trees, and the rich, damp smell from the garden filled me with a restless excitement.

It was as if something waited out there in the rain beyond the lamplight, although for the life of me I could not even guess at what it might be.

2 GLORIA

In order to avoid being called a flirt she always yielded easily.

—Charles, Count Talleyrand

The following day being a Saturday, I decided to follow Jake's advice without delay. The sports jacket and flannels which were the sole survivors of my pre-army wardrobe were completely unwearable, and on my release group number I had not been entitled to a demobilization suit.

It seemed to me that this was no bad thing, for as Jake had indicated there were certain advantages to a uniform, and I was entitled to continue wearing it until the end of my release leave.

It looked remarkably well after a careful press, particularly the sergeant's stripes and the Berlin insignia, a dark circle ringed with red to indicate a besieged city and affectionately referred to by the troops as "the flaming arsehole."

But that and the green flash of the Intelligence Corps were not the only splashes of color to be seen, for I was the proud possessor of the General Service Medal (Palestine 1945–48) thanks to that month in the transit camp at Jaffa. The purple-green-purple ribbon looked rather well above the left breast pocket, and there was always the remote chance that to the uninitiated it might be mistaken for a decoration for valor.

The army, in its wisdom, had released me with five pounds against the eventuality of the records' proving that I owed them money, any surplus credits to be paid at their convenience. It left me distinctly on the short side financially so I adjusted my beret to a rakish angle and went to see Aunt Alice.

I found her in the drawing room working her way through a book on astral projection. The housecoat she was wearing had been in her possession for many years, and she invariably wore it when indoors, especially when she was in what she termed her mystical moods. It was embroidered with the signs of the zodiac and, combined with jet-black hair hanging straight to her shoulders, made her resemble the high priestess of some strange cult.

She was at that time a plump, bosomy woman in her middle fifties. Her father had left her eight or nine houses in various parts of the town, most of them split into flats, and the rent from these had enabled her to live in tolerable comfort for many years. She had looked after me with considerable kindness since I was eight, and I was extremely fond of her.

I explained my present predicament, then spent a good ten minutes searching for her handbag, which finally turned out to be under the cushion of the chair she was sitting on. She offered me a ten-shilling note, which I accepted in spite of the fact that I'd been hoping for a pound, and I went in search of Uncle Herbert to spread the load.

As I'd expected, I found him in the conservatory in his baize apron and old straw boater, contentedly potting plants at the bench. He had never worked for a living in the usual sense in all the years I had known him, had never ventured once beyond the garden gate. But there were reasons.

On July 1, 1916, Uncle Herbert had gone over the top on the Somme with seven hundred and seventy-three officers and men of one of the Yorkshire Pals regiments. Twenty minutes later, the heavy machine guns having done their work, he found himself one of thirty-four survivors, albeit with two bullets in one leg and another in the throat.

And so he had lived on all these years, the voice a bare whisper when he used it at all, the left leg permanently supported in a steel brace.

This time the money situation was reversed. I requested ten shillings and had a pound note thrust upon me. As any kind of conversation tired him excessively, I kept my thanks to a minimum and left him to his potting. A nice little man who never strayed far from the safety of the orchids in his greenhouse. A pale ghost in the evening sunlight.

. . .

I had been to a dance or two during my army service, but not many, and those mainly mess brawls with too few girls to go around and too much to drink.

In spite of that, I was capable of getting around the floor without disgracing myself, thanks to a series of Saturday-night hops at the local church hall when I was sixteen. As I remember, it was all as clean as a whistle, mainly boy scouts and girl guides in their Sunday best, with the vicar behind a trestle table dispensing lemonade at the interval. And then Wilma turned up.

She was an entirely different proposition from the rest of the females. For one thing, she was twenty and looked older—a real woman with long blond hair and a figure to thank God for, or at least that's how I remember her.

She was too good. Hardly any of the boys danced with her. They didn't have the nerve. I only did myself as a dare. They were playing a slow foxtrot number from *Casablanca* with Humphrey Bogart, "As Time Goes By." To this day, whenever I hear that tune, I feel her arm sliding behind my neck, her body pressing against me on the turns.

It seemed impossible that such a queen among women could be interested in me, and yet I found myself walking her home through the perfumed darkness, shaking with excitement at the very thought of being with her.

A short cut to her home lay across the school playing fields. We paused in a small wood at the edge. I kissed her clumsily. After a while, we sat on a pile of dead leaves and I attempted further liberties.

She pushed my eager hands away at once and told me not to spoil things. She seemed angry and I thought I'd gone too far. She offered me a cigarette, which I accepted eagerly, for they were hard to come by at that stage of the war.

I sat smoking the cigarette, inhaling deeply, for I had already discovered the pleasures of nicotine. Wilma sat quietly for a moment, then leaned forward suddenly and unbuttoned my trousers. I reached for her at once and she pushed me away instantly. "No," she said firmly, then started to play with me with slow, capable fingers.

I lay back against the leaves, inhaling deeply until my head buzzed, alternating between the twin delights of tobacco and sexual pleasure. This performance became something of a ritual with us and never varied in the slightest detail except on occasion as regarded the brand of cigarette, and I was never permitted the slightest intimacy as far as she was concerned.

A strange business. Even stranger was the way it ended, for she simply didn't turn up to meet me one night. A week later, when I saw her by chance on a tram, she looked through me as if she had never set eyes on me in her life. Perhaps I had served her purpose in some strange way.

• • •

Of all the dance halls I patronized during that year, the Trocadero was my favorite—a Moorish palace that would not have disgraced a Hollywood film set, thanks to the wild fantasy of the man who had created it, incongruously set down on a main road three miles out from the city center in a respectable middle-class suburb.

There was music on the night air that first evening. It drew me like a magnet when I came out of the public bar of The Tall Man, where I had paused to take in two statutory pints of best bitter to fortify me for the fray, and I hurried down the road toward the red neon glow in the darkness beyond the trees.

I was dismayed by the size of the queue stretching out through the main door, for it was only eight o'clock; but as I discovered later, this was usual on a Saturday night, for numbers were strictly limited according to some city bylaw or other. I stood in the rain in an agony of impatience, the queue building up behind me, inching forward for fifteen minutes or so until I was finally inside the door.

There were only five or six people between me and the glass window now, but for the moment no more tickets were being issued. We waited under the inscrutable stares of a posse of four or five commissionaires—burly gentlemen in smart green uniforms, medal ribbons prominently displayed, sergeant majors to the last man, ready to move in at the first sign of trouble, for the Trocadero prided itself on its respectability and orderliness.

The glass doors on the other side of the foyer swung open, giving a tantalizing glimpse of the crowd inside as the band struck up a quickstep. The manager came through in his prewar dinner jacket and boiled shirt, leaned down to the ticket window and murmured something to the girl inside. We moved forward with a rush. I shoved my three shillings across and received my ticket, which was immediately taken from me by one of the commissionaires.

There was a chorus of groans as the doors were closed behind on those unfortunates who still waited in the rain. My luck was good, or so it seemed to me then, and I went excitedly up the stairs to the cloakroom.

. . .

I got rid of my greatcoat, moved out onto the balcony that ran around each side of the dance floor and leaned on the rail. There were two eight-piece bands, each on its own stand, red tuxedos on one side of the hall, blue on the other. They played alternately, never together, for there was considerable rivalry between them. Just now, the reds were playing "Tuxedo Junction," the lights were low and two great glass balls turned slowly in the ceiling, waves of scarlet, blue and green rippling across the heads of the dancers.

The music stopped, the lights were turned up again and the floor started to clear in the hiatus between one band's finishing and the other continuing the good work.

It was time. I lit a cigarette, moved to the head of the stairs and paused to check my appearance in the full-length mirror. The uniform really looked very good indeed, and the medal ribbon was all that could be desired. I assumed a suitably cynical expression, pulled my hair down across my eyes for no satisfactory reason and descended the stairs.

I paused a few steps from the bottom and looked into the crowd, hands in pockets, cigarette dangling from the corner of my mouth, a world-weary young veteran home from the wars, an object of pity and admiration to every woman in the room, or so I fondly imagined.

• • •

The truth is that the whole thing was something of an anticlimax. No one took the slightest notice of me. Indeed, why should they? I was just another face in the crowd, and few human beings really look at each other anyway, a lesson to be learned painfully over a considerable number of years.

In any event, I was "spoilt for choice," as they say in Yorkshire. It was rather like being in some gigantic store with the entire range of the product displayed in all its infinite variety. Fat, thin, blond or brunette, from the downright ugly to the ravishingly beautiful. You name it, they had it, and in large quantities, for the women far outnumbered the men.

Something else that didn't help was the fact that I was slightly shortsighted. The only pair of spectacles I possessed were army issue: round-lensed, steel-framed and of a type favored by Heinrich Himmler, Chief of the Gestapo, which was hardly the image I was trying to create. I preferred to manage without, which meant that at anything like a distance, faces softened slightly, blurred at the edges, especially when the lights were low. Good-looking girls, on closer inspection, often proved to be quite plain or worse and the reverse was equally true.

The first girl I asked to dance was an example of this. I was attracted by the red-gold hair, which turned out to be purely an effect of the light when I was too close to turn away. She was also incredibly fat, something else which had not been apparent because of the crush surrounding us.

The band was playing a waltz at the time, and manhandling her around the floor was a task that might well have taxed even Charles Atlas in his prime. She didn't say a word during the entire proceedings, simply hung on tight, a great, bovine grin on her face, apparently oblivious to the sweat that had soaked through her blouse in large patches.

At the end of the number, I fled to the balcony café where I revived myself with a cigarette and a cup of tea before returning to the fray. The balcony, in fact, was a good place from which to spy out the land, and if you worked your way around it slowly, it was possible to cover every part of the room.

There was a blond girl standing at the side of the reds' bandstand. I couldn't help noticing her, for the crowd seemed to have thinned out at that point and she was quite alone. She wore a green dress, and when I slipped on my spectacles furtively to get an accurate reading, I discovered that she was really very pretty indeed.

I hurried downstairs and pushed my way through the crowd, fearful that she would be gone before I arrived, but my luck was good, for she still stood there by the bandstand, quite alone.

I moved in without hesitation and asked her to dance, and the smile I received was all that could be desired. She fitted her body into mine, every melting curve, and we drifted out onto the floor as the lights faded into a blue mist and the band eased into the smoothest of foxtrots.

A Foggy Day in London Town. I'll never forget it for it still brings back that first wild feeling of elation at my unbelievable luck, followed immediately by a rapid slide down into a species of living hell, for within seconds I was enveloped in a kind of miasma that had to be experienced to be believed.

I had heard of body odor, had experienced it on occasion in both the male and female varieties. But this was something special—worthy of inclusion in any medical textbook.

She had one thing in common with the fat girl, which was a complete absence of conversation. The generous mouth stayed parted in a ready smile, and she fastened each available inch of her more than adequate body into mine like a limpet to a rock without the slightest evidence that she ever intended to let go.

Hell on earth would be a less than adequate description, and I drifted around the floor in a kind of daze, holding on to my sanity with everything I had. When the first number came to an end, I mumbled some wild and improbable excuse and fled, leaving her there on the floor.

I made it to the other side of the stairs where I could breathe clean air, and lit a cigarette with trembling hands. It occurred to me then that the evening was fast disintegrating, and that would never do. I glanced about me wildly and grabbed the nearest unattached female by the arm, a small, neat redhead.

Perhaps I was too rough, or, what is even more probable, some hint of my previous partner still clung to me. The girl in question held me at arm's length, her face averted, while we circled the floor three or four times. The moment the music came to an end, she left me to make my own way to the edge of the floor. It was enough. I went to the foyer, obtained a pass and rushed coatless through the rain to the sanctuary of The Tall Man.

The bar, as was to be expected at that time on a Saturday night, was crowded. I finally managed to order a pint and retreated to a corner by the window beside a group of six or seven young men of my own age, all wearing the blazer of the local rugby club.

One of them turned to stub out a cigarette and jogged my elbow. I recognized him at once as an old schoolfellow, if not friend. I remembered him as a boy of infinite vulgarity, a pest on the field and off, whose main delight had been a preoccupation with grabbing at one's balls in the showers after a match. As I recalled, he had possessed only one talent, an ability to break wind at will, a rather infantile pastime but a source of considerable personal pleasure to him, particularly when lady teachers were taking the form. He had been known quite simply as Dirty George.

From the way he acted it would have been reasonable to suppose I was his oldest and dearest friend, encountered by chance at a distance of years, but I had never much cared for the rugby crowd, declined his offer of a drink and got out of there as fast as I could.

· · ·

Presumably my confidence must have been shaken for, as I recall, the rest of the evening was a complete disaster. When I returned to the Trocadero I moved aimlessly through the crowd, apparently incapable of summoning up the courage to ask any girl to dance again.

Suddenly it was five past eleven, and the place closed at eleven-thirty. I stood at the bottom of the stairs, down to my last two cigarettes, the evening in ruins, when I became aware that Dirty George was standing beside me.

"Hello, old man," he said. "Wondered where you'd got to. Having any luck?" I shook my head glumly. He nodded sympathetically, his eyes wandering around the floor, and suddenly an alert expression appeared on his face. He touched my arm. "Now there's a dead cert if you like."

He nodded toward the blues' bandstand, and I saw a girl leaning against a pillar. She was perhaps eighteen and had very dark hair cut close to her head. The skirt of her blue dress was only knee-length, and she wore platform shoes with ankle straps, the whole combining with the rather sullen orange mouth to remind me excitingly of Ava.

"Are you sure?" I said.

"You can't go wrong, old man," he assured me solemnly.

I plowed through the crowd at once and touched her elbow. "Care to dance?"

She examined me briefly, then nodded. "If you like," she said casually.

I knew I was on to a good thing the moment I took hold of her. It was not just the bodily contact, although there was plenty of that, my knee moving between her thighs on each turn in the quickstep. The big thing was that she had a faint air of corruption about her. A suggestion of that fantasy figure who features in most men's dreams at one time or another—the tart who will do anything she's told to do.

Good old Dirty George. As the number came to an end I said brightly, "Who's taking you home?"

Her brows lifted fractionally and there was a new look in her eyes. "You don't waste any time, do you?"

"Never could see the point," I told her and slipped a cigarette into the corner of my mouth, Bogart to the life. "What's your name?"

"Gloria," she said. "I'll get my coat now and beat the rush. See you at the main door."

She faded into the crowd and I moved toward the stairs where Dirty George was standing with one of his green-blazered rugby pals. They were laughing hugely together at some private joke.

I slapped him on the back, full of goodwill. "Thanks. I'll do the same for you some time."

The smile faded and he stared at me in astonishment. "You mean you got off with her?"

"Just like you said," I told him. "A dead cert."

He seemed bereft of speech for a moment, and when he spoke, it was in a kind of hoarse whisper. "But I was only kidding, old man. Never clapped eyes on her in my life before."

Which was really very funny. I patted him on the shoulder gently. "It only goes to prove, George," I said solemnly, "that all is for the best in the best of all possible worlds."

I left him there, considerably shaken, and went upstairs to the cloakroom.

• • •

There had to be a snag, of course, and it was waiting for me in the foyer in the person of a tall, rather plain girl in a brown tweed coat and a head scarf whom Gloria introduced as her sister, Pam. I didn't mind if she walked home with us, did I? I managed a ready smile, but only just, and followed them outside.

The rain had developed into a hard, persistent downpour and looked as if it had settled in for the rest of the month. Gloria had an umbrella with her which she and her sister shared, and I turned up the collar of my coat, pulled my beret down over my eyes and trailed miserably in their wake.

We followed the main road for about a mile, the two girls discussing a film they'd seen together the previous night, making no attempt to include me in the conversation. On several occasions I was tempted to simply creep away, for I had the distinct impression that I would hardly be missed. The whole thing, by then, seemed a colossal waste of time. Finally we turned off the main road into a corporation-housing estate and moved into a cul-de-sac of semidetached houses.

Gloria opened a gate and started along a narrow concrete path, her sister at her shoulder. I followed for no good reason that I could see, for she had still not spoken to me. At the rear of the house there was a small patch of lawn and a concrete porch with a light over it. There was also a light in the kitchen although the curtains were drawn.

The girls paused on the porch. Gloria closed her umbrella, shaking it vigorously, and Pam turned to me. To my utter amazement, she smiled brightly. "Thanks for bringing me home, Jack," she said, opened the kitchen door and went inside, closing it again.

I turned to Gloria, my heart in my mouth, and

reached out for her. She said calmly, "We'll go in the greenhouse, if you like. It's warm in there. My dad leaves an oil heater on nights."

In the same instant, the kitchen door was flung open and a wild-eyed youth with long, narrow sideburns punched me in the face.

•   •   •

I have never been much of a fighting man in spite of the army's attempts to teach me the rudiments of unarmed combat. Let's say I was perfectly well aware of the theory of the thing. It was just that I balked at putting it into practice.

In this case, I didn't have much choice, if only for reasons of self-preservation. His fist grazed my cheek as he shouted incoherently, and I moved in close and tried to throw him over my hip in the approved manner. We went down together in an untidy heap, rolling about on the lawn in the rain with him trying to punch my head in.

But help was at hand. There was Gloria's umbrella, Pam's handbag with which she came out of the kitchen to flail my assailant unmercifully about the head, and a small, bullet-headed man in shirt-sleeves, who finally hauled him off me.

Gloria helped me to my feet while the other two sorted out Sideburns. "Stupid, jealous bastard!" I heard Pam say, and then she and the gentleman in shirt-sleeves hustled him inside and closed the door.

I wiped mud from my face with my handkerchief. Gloria said calmly, "He's a jealous devil, is Ronnie. Can't stand the idea of anyone seeing our Pam home. They had a row last Sunday so she wouldn't go out with him tonight," she added by way of further explanation.

"But I didn't bring her home," I said in bewilderment. "Not the way you mean, anyway."

"But he thought you did," she said. "Gets in a blind rage when he's in that mood. Only sees what he wants to see."

By this time the whole business had taken on the aspect of some privileged nightmare, especially when she added, with a touch of impatience, "Come on, let's go into the greenhouse if we're going. I'm getting soaked."

My cheek was beginning to hurt where he'd punched me, but it didn't seem to matter in the warm, paraffin-smelling darkness with the rain pattering against the glass roof.

Gloria leaned back against the wooden door, strangely indifferent as I unbuttoned her coat, my heart thumping, and pulled her against me. When I kissed her, it was not that her mouth was unresponsive. It was simply neutral in a curious way, and yet she allowed me to caress her body at will. Finally, greatly daring, I slipped both hands beneath her skirt. I stayed there for a while holding her, my body trembling, perilously close to the point of explosion.

She said impatiently, "For God's sake, don't be all night about it."

I peered at her in puzzlement, her face a dim shadow in the light of the small oil lamp. "What did you say?"

"Are you going to have it or aren't you?" she demanded, then pushed me away quite violently and picked up her handbag and umbrella. "Honestly, I don't know why I bother. You're all the same. It's all you ever want and it doesn't mean a damn thing to me."

She opened the door and pushed me outside, and I went meekly, utterly bewildered by this new vagary of female behavior. When we reached the porch, she said roughly, "We'll say good night, then," and disappeared inside.

So that was very much that. I went out through the gate, down the cul-de-sac toward the main road, and started the long walk home through the heavy rain.

• • •

The light was on in Jake's room above the garage in spite of the lateness of the hour and I found him sitting by the fire reading a book. He made a fresh pot of tea, and I dried myself by the hearth and recounted the evening's events with some bewilderment.

"Poor Oliver," he said. "You've certainly had a night of it."

"But what in the hell was she playing at?" I demanded.

"God knows." He shrugged. "The female of the species comes in all shapes and sizes, old sport. Some of them just don't take to the flesh at all."

"More likely she just didn't take to me," I said morosely. "What in the hell did she expect, anyway?"

"She probably thought you'd have it off in your trousers like a good boy and depart into the night, satisfied."

"The bitch," I said.

43

"What you need, Oliver, is a good woman to take you in hand. Someone who's been around long enough to know what it's all about."

"And just where am I supposed to find someone like that?"

He smiled. "Try the Trocadero next Tuesday or Wednesday. Nothing like as crowded as Saturdays. It's cheaper, too."

"Why should I be any more successful then than I've been tonight?" I asked him.

"Oh, you get a different brand of customer during the week. Give it a try. You'll see what I mean."

I thought about what he had said as I walked home through the rain-soaked garden, and later, sitting by the open window of my bedroom, smoking my last cigarette. I was tired, my face hurt, but I felt surprisingly cheerful. At least I'd had an adventure of sorts, which was something, and tomorrow, or to be more specific, next Tuesday, had a kind of infinite promise to it.

I went to bed, well content.

3 HELEN

Sooner or later what every young boy needs is a good woman to take him in hand.

—Anon

The following Monday, the whole world changed with the morning post. The first letter was important enough, in its way, a check for one hundred and three pounds thirteen shillings from the army in settlement of all debts. But the second was the big surprise—a communication from the University of London to inform me of my success in the final examinations which I had sat for as an external student earlier in the year.

Without any false modesty, I can truly say that I

had never expected to pass, for sociology and social psychology had never particularly interested me. The only reason I had started the course in the first place was that the insurance firm I'd worked for before joining up had offered two afternoons off each week on full pay at the local college, and in those days I was willing to do anything to get out of the office. I'd only bothered to take my finals because the army had offered what they termed compassionate leave to come home to take the examinations, a chance not to be missed.

But now, for good or ill, I was a Bachelor of Science with third class honors, thanks to failing a compulsory paper in statistics, which had reduced me a class. I gave Jake a ring at his office to impart the good news and arranged to have lunch with him. He had only an hour so we adjourned to a pub around the corner from his place and ordered beer and sandwiches.

We sat in a booth and he toasted me solemnly. "To you, old sport. I think it's bloody marvelous. The thing is, now you've got it, what are you going to do with it?"

"God knows," I said. "I never expected to pass."

"They'll probably offer you a promotion if you go back to the old firm now," he said.

I shook my head firmly. "That's out for a start. I'll never work in an office again as long as I live. That's a promise."

"How long have you been writing now?"

"Since I was thirteen."

"And never sold a word."

"All right," I said with some feeling, for it was the

one area in my life that was really of importance to me. "Don't rub it in."

"I didn't intend to. Simply wanted to make the point that you can't expect to make a living in that quarter, or at least not for some time."

I sat there rather glumly, thinking it over, and he went to get two more beers. When he returned, he was frowning thoughtfully. "What about teaching?" he said as he sat down.

I stared at him blankly. "Teaching? But I haven't got any training, you know that."

"You don't need any," he said and swallowed some of his beer. "A client of ours was telling me there's such a shortage of teachers these days, they'll take anybody. As long as they've got a degree, that is."

It didn't seem very probable to me. I said, "Are you sure?"

He nodded, "Oh, yes, as long as you've got a degree, they'll take you without teacher training."

"Any degree?"

"Apparently. You could do worse, you know. Nine to four, twelve weeks' holiday a year. Leave you plenty of time to write." He swallowed the rest of the beer and stood up. "I'll have to run. See you later. I'd give it some thought if I were you."

Which I did, with the aid of another pint, finally phoning the local education offices from the call box in the corner of the bar—and with a promptness I should have recognized as suspicious in any branch of local government, I was invited for an interview at three o'clock that very afternoon.

• • •

The interview, if such it can be termed, was conducted by Messrs. Crosby and Dawson, two of the most genial men I'd ever met in my life. Too genial, in fact. The blunt truth was that I simply didn't realize how scarce teachers were at that time, particularly in the industrial north.

From their first firm handshake to their exclamations of ecstasy on examining the letter from London University confirming my new status, they were entirely on my side. In fact, for most of the time they discussed me solemnly as if I were not there, extolling my scholarship and other virtues to a degree that would have proved embarrassing had it not been so ridiculously extravagant.

In the end, after much apparent perusal of various files, they announced that they would be happy to offer me a temporary appointment as an assistant master for a probationary year at a salary of thirty-three pounds, ten shillings and twopence per calendar month.

Which seemed reasonable enough. I filled in the necessary form and signed it. Mr. Crosby pulled it away from me with what I can only describe as indecent haste. His smile, as he cast his eye over it, seemed just a trifle more formal than before.

"And when would my duties commence?" I inquired.

"Next Monday, I think." He took the card that Dawson passed him from a box file. "We have an excellent post for you here. Most suitable. Couldn't be better. You are familiar with the Bagley area of the city?"

I was indeed. One of the roughest slums on the wrong side of the river. I nodded, my heart sinking a little, and he passed the card across. "The address is on there. Mr. Carter's the man to see. One of our most able headmasters. If you've time, I suggest you pop along and see him at close of school today."

I examined the card slowly. "Khyber Street Secondary Modern School."

He smiled blandly. "I'm sure you'll have a great deal to offer to older boys and girls, Mr. Shaw, a man of your experience."

• • •

The full horror of it didn't hit me until I saw the school, although the district itself was bad enough with its cobbled streets and wretched little back-to-back terraces, the lavatories grouped together in small yards halfway along every street, each one serving four houses.

The school was a grim, forbidding building of brick and stone, well blackened by the years, and gave a rather curious impression of height, mainly, I think, because the best use had had to be made of a rather small site. It certainly towered above the roofs of the surrounding houses and reminded me of some Dickensian workhouse more than anything else, which was hardly surprising. Originally it had been what was known in the trade as a board school, a product of that sudden late-Victorian interest in educating the workers.

Beyond the fringe of green-painted iron railings was a rather small asphalt playground with toilets in one corner. There were two entrances at each end of the main building, the sexes being strictly segregated.

I pushed open the door marked "Boys" and found myself in a dark hall at the bottom of a flight of stairs. There was a vaguely unpleasant smell, possibly from the dustbins ranged against the wall beside a door.

I hesitated, the door opened, and a man in a brown coverall appeared and emptied a shovelful of wood shavings into one of the bins. He looked at me inquiringly, a small, wiry fox terrier of a man, with iron-gray hair that fell untidily across his eyes. Beyond his shoulder I could see a sullen-looking youth in shirt-sleeves planing a plank of wood at a bench.

I asked him for the headmaster's office and he directed me in a dry West Riding voice. I thanked him, and as I turned away he flicked the shoulder flash on my battle-dress sleeve. "Intelligence, eh? By gum, lad, but we could do with some of that around here."

He went back into the woodwork room and I went up the steps. The walls were covered with white tiles which, coupled with the smell, reminded me depressingly of a public urinal.

On the next landing I found two boys lounging against the wall opposite the headmaster's door, their heads together over some health magazine or other, nude ladies baring their bosoms to God's good air. The magazine disappeared into the pocket of a shabby tweed jacket a couple of sizes too large for its owner, a burly-looking lad of perhaps fourteen, with ginger hair and a face that seemed all low cunning.

"I'm looking for Mr. Carter," I said.

"In the office, sir."

He spoke with a hard nasal twang and with apparent politeness, and yet the insolence about an eighth of an inch beneath the surface had to be heard to be believed. Most sinister of all, I noticed that the belt around his waist was heavily studded with army badges. His companion, a vacuous youth in a torn jersey, head shaven except for a tuft of hair above the forehead, stared at me, a candle of snot descending from one nostril. *Thirty-three pounds, ten shillings and twopence a month.* I turned to the door hurriedly and knocked.

There was no reply. I knocked again, was aware of a sudden flurry of movement, and then the door was flung open violently. "Didn't I tell you to wait, boy?"

The voice had a parade-ground roar perfected over the years by necessity, one supposed, for Mr. Carter was a small man. His face was wrinkled and tinged with yellow, even the bald head, so that he had the perpetual look of a man recovering from a severe attack of jaundice. He wore wire-rimmed glasses and held a cigarette in the exact center of his mouth. His upper lip was brown with nicotine.

A ready smile replaced the frown, sunshine through the clouds. "Mr. Shaw, I presume?"

"That's right," I said.

He drew me inside, sternly ordering my two friends outside to await his pleasure. His office walls were adorned with the same white tiles as the corridor outside. For the first time I could appreciate what they meant by the term "neo-lavatorial architecture."

There were several filing cabinets, an untidy desk, a shabby carpet, a pint pot redolent of guardhouse days beside an electric kettle. Beyond, through the window, I could see the roofs of those mean little houses. The whole thing was unbelievably depressing, including Mr. Carter. He lit another cigarette from the stub of the one in his mouth and, wreathed in smoke, sat down behind his desk, his words punctuated by a series of graveyard coughs.

Mr. Crosby had phoned him from the education offices to warn him that I was coming and had obviously managed to convey his own ecstatic delight in their good fortune at getting me, for Mr. Carter was just as delighted. His extravagant regard for someone he had never met in his life before filled me with astonishment, but as I discovered later he simply couldn't believe his luck at being offered another man, any man, after the school year had started.

"We'll be delighted to have a graduate on the staff," he commented at one stage in the conversation.

I pointed out that I had no teacher training. More than that, no experience whatsoever.

He frowned. "You do have a degree, don't you?" There hasn't been any mistake?"

"Yes, but it's in sociology, social psychology, philosophy."

His brow cleared. "That's all right then"—an attitude which mystified me less after my first few months in teaching, for I had by then encountered, among general class teachers, a man with a degree in brewing engineering, another with a M.Sc. in textiles, having specialized particularly in the area of ropes and cordage, and a delectable Eurasian lady with a law degree.

On the question of future duties, Mr. Carter proved not only vague, but evasive. All would be taken care of in God's good time, and he looked forward to seeing me on Monday morning at ten to nine.

When he opened the door to usher me out, my two friends at the wall had a smaller boy between them and were twisting an arm apiece.

"Varley!" roared Mr. Carter. "How many times have I told you?"

The ginger boy ducked expertly and the headmaster's fist connected with his companion's face. He drove them toward the stairs, striking indiscriminately at each head, including that of the wretched little boy who had been the object of the bullying.

They disappeared into the gloom below and he turned and said solemnly, "Grand lads, Mr. Shaw. Grand lads, really, all of them."

He shook hands and disappeared back into his office.

The woodwork instructor was standing at his open door lighting a pipe when I went downstairs. He looked at me inquiringly and I held out my hand.

"Oliver Shaw. I'm joining you Monday."

"God help you," he said and went back inside the woodwork room.

There was a small transport café on the other side of the street. I ordered a cup of tea and sat at the window staring across at the school, hoping in some strange way that if I looked at it long enough I might get used to it.

I heard the four o'clock bell quite clearly. The

first person out the door was the woodwork instructor in shabby raincoat and trilby, clutching a briefcase. Within seconds, a steady stream of boys boiled after him, with here and there an adult or two bobbing helplessly, presumably the other teachers.

Finally, Mr. Carter himself appeared, a gray topcoat over his arm. The yard by then was quite deserted, and he looked relaxed and happy as he went through the gate. I checked my watch. It was exactly five minutes past four.

• • •

I went into town the following morning to get some new clothes. There were no difficulties; clothes rationing had ended earlier that year. A pair of flannels and a Donegal tweed sports jacket seemed the right sort of thing for Khyber Street. For more formal occasions, I chose a double-breasted suit of dark-blue worsted in the new drape style, the latest import from America.

I really looked rather well as I dressed that evening before leaving for the Trocadero. I adjusted the Windsor knot in my tie, gave my hair a final comb, and went in search of Aunt Alice to settle my few debts with her.

I found her in the drawing room in the company of a large, Teutonic-looking gentleman wearing a pince-nez, with hair like a brush top. He stood up and clicked his heels when she introduced him.

"This is Herr Nagel, dear, he's doing your horoscope."

I was not particularly dismayed at this item of news for Aunt Alice usually had some such creature in tow, and although she had a particular penchant for mediums, astrology was an old love. He shook hands, exposing gold-capped teeth in a frozen smile before sitting and returning to his labors. He was, as I discovered later, a German Jew who had got out of Berlin by the skin of his teeth just before the war.

She asked me where I was going and when I told her, she shook her head, a serious look on her face. "Oh, dear, that's bad. Isn't that bad, Conrad?" Here she appealed to Herr Nagel, who glanced up dutifully. "Oliver's going dancing," she explained.

"So what?" I said.

"Is that wise in view of what you said about his relations with the opposite sex?" Aunt Alice said to Herr Nagel. She patted my hand. "It's in your map, you see, dear."

I turned inquiringly to Herr Nagel as enlightenment dawned on his face like a sunburst.

"Ah, vimmen!" he said. "Now I understand."

He got up and walked about the room, his pincenez in one hand, the other under his coattails, grinding his teeth together, speaking slowly and with considerable drama in a manner which, coupled with his accent, would hardly have disgraced Erich von Stroheim playing a Gestapo chief.

"Among your aspects, young man, you haff Venus squared mit Mars, which means that you will meet with more than your fair share of unkindness from the opposite sex."

He paused to savor that last word, which was obviously a favorite, and he rolled it sibilantly around his tongue, one hand on Aunt Alice's shoulder, before continuing.

"For you, my boy, the ideal never works out in reality. I do not say that a happy marriage vill not come, for you haff Jupiter in the House of Marriage, unt the Moon in goot aspect mit Venus."

I glanced helplessly at Aunt Alice. "But what's it all supposed to mean?"

"You tend to put them on a pedestal, mein young friend, that's vot it means." He put a hand on my shoulder. "Unt they always fall off. Sad, isn't it?"

He apparently found this funny and laughed uproariously. So did Aunt Alice, which seemed to be the signal for him to take her hand, kiss it passionately and click his heels.

I withdrew, found an old trench coat in the hall wardrobe in case of rain and let myself out of the front door, whistling cheerfully, for I didn't believe a word of it, or at least, not enough to let it spoil my evening.

• • •

The Trocadero that Tuesday evening was everything Jake had promised. There was room to breathe, to move about the floor. I don't suppose there could have been more than three hundred people in the place, which meant that it seemed half empty.

Only one band was on duty, the reds, as it happened, and a great deal of serious ballroom dancing was going on when I came out of the cloakroom and looked down from the balcony. As usual, there were more females in evidence than males, but the clientele seemed different—on the whole a little older, more serious. The girls seemed to look my way more often, although that was perhaps imagination or, quite simply, the new suit.

As before, I needed to make an entrance, if only for my own private sake, as if to assure myself that I was somehow in control. I paused before the mirror at the top of the stairs for a final check. The drape suit with those trousers about half a yard wide made me look like a young Robert Mitchum, or so I fondly imagined. I hooded my eyes and stuck a cigarette in the corner of my mouth.

When I turned, I was disconcerted to find myself the object of some amusement for a young woman who had just appeared from the cloakroom. She was hardly dressed for dancing in a suit of orange tweed with a rather prim skirt, and neat brown brogues. Her black hair, which was tied in a bun, framed a pale oval face, dark eyes, very little lipstick.

The smile would best be described as one of gentle amusement, not mockery, but I turned away in confusion and stumbled down the stairs.

· · ·

The older I get, the more convinced I am that time and chance have more of a hand in a man's affairs than is generally realized, especially where matters of import are concerned. Take that first meeting with Helen, for example, one of the most important of my life. It was a miracle that we ever got together at all.

First, there was the circumstance that brought her out of the cloakroom at exactly the right moment to catch me, naked, in a manner of speaking, in front of that mirror. I know now that it was my vulnerability which immediately attracted her. Yet for me, the shame of it was such that I could not have walked up to her and asked her to dance for a hundred pounds.

In any case, she wasn't the sort I was looking for

at all. Far too prim and ladylike, and she was too old for me. She admitted, at a later stage, to twenty-eight, but I am sure now that she was older than that.

So everything was against us until the bandleader announced that the next number would be a ladies' choice, an event which took place only rarely, and certainly not every night. Surprisingly, few girls availed themselves of the opportunity, presumably for reasons of maidenly modesty. It was a great thing to be asked at all, and most men waited, chatting with friends, with every evidence of unconcern.

But, as the Bible has it, few were chosen, and I was one of them. I was aware of the tug at my arm and turned to find the woman in the orange tweed suit from the balcony.

"May I have this dance?" she asked in a low, sweet voice.

I swallowed my confusion and followed her onto the floor. Everything about her was wrong. The neat clothes, the madonnalike face, that beautifully modulated voice, and yet, when I took her in my arms, my heart started to pound, my stomach contracted, the inside of my mouth went dry.

That two members of the opposite sex can strike sparks from each other from the first meeting without even a word being spoken is a common enough phenomenon, and frequently such passion has nothing to do with love in the usual sense of the word. Something inexplicable happens and two people come together inexorably.

To hold her in my arms, even lightly, was the most exciting thing that had ever happened to me. They were playing an old early-thirties number recently revived, "Put Your Head on My Shoulder." She did just that, one hand up around the back of my neck, dancing as intimately as it was possible to get.

From the beginning, then, there was an inevitability to it all. When the dance ended, she allowed her hand to stay in mine as if it were the most natural thing in the world. I can't even recall asking her to have coffee with me. I believe we just went.

We sat at a balcony table, drank coffee, smoked cigarettes, watched the dancing below and talked, heads together, in a low, intimate way, like lovers who, having been long parted, had much to tell each other. And that, I recall at a distance of time, was the strangest thing of all, for it was as if I had always known her in spite of the fact that in the end I never really knew her at all.

I cannot remember when we exchanged names; in retrospect, she was Helen from that very first moment, but I do know that I talked of myself as I had never talked to anyone other than Jake. The army, my writing, teaching, future hopes and past disappointments. Of herself she had strangely little to say, and nothing of a very revealing nature, although this, too, only became apparent later. I remember her saying that she was private secretary to a solicitor in the town, no more than that.

We danced again after a while, "September Song," the world a blue mist, the glass ball in the ceiling casting great, rippling waves across us, and once, and this was the only time she did such a thing publicly, she pulled down my head and kissed me, her mouth soft and warm, opening like a flower, a kiss like no other I had ever had before.

And then it was over and we were outside, walking together through a light drizzle beneath her umbrella. I had asked to take her home, but she had named a suburb four or five miles on the far side of town, had insisted firmly that I take her only as far as the tram stop on the main road.

We walked slowly along the wet pavement, pausing occasionally to kiss. I asked her to go out with me one evening. The cinema or just a walk, perhaps. Anything. She shook her head firmly. It just wasn't possible. She was too busy with prior commitments.

The frustration was terrible and explains, I suppose, what followed. We were standing on the corner of a small, dark alley. I grabbed her elbow rather roughly and pushed her into the shadows. Then I crushed her to me and kissed her hard, forcing her head back.

She broke away from me, slightly breathless, shaking a little as she reached up to touch my face. "No, Oliver, not now. Not this way. There's no need."

A remark which naturally made not the slightest sense to me, and I grabbed her again, caressing her right breast clumsily.

I got a good old-fashioned slap in the face that sent me back across the alley. She moved into the circle of light cast by a gas lamp and paused to rearrange herself, her face pale, yet calm as she glanced once toward me before walking away.

The immediate feeling was one of panic, sheer, blind panic at the thought of losing her. I acted purely by reflex, running after her instantly and falling into step beside her. I couldn't think of anything worth the saying, but I mumbled something about wanting to see her to the tram stop. At least she didn't say no, and we continued together in silence.

I have seldom felt more miserable in my life than I did standing in the rain with her at the end of a small queue. She hadn't said a word, simply started to move out of my life forever, when the tram came and the queue started forward. There was a lump in my throat the size of a fist. I could have cried like a child. I plucked at her sleeve instinctively as she reached for the handrail.

"I'm sorry," I said.

"Good," she said calmly. "A little suffering now and then is good for the soul."

I started to turn away, and as the tram moved off, she was standing at the edge of the platform, hanging on to the handrail. "The Trocadero, Thursday." she called. "Seven-thirty. I'll see you inside."

It was like a miracle. So great was the release of energy that instead of catching a tram myself in the opposite direction, I walked through the rain for a good mile and a half, feeling incredibly cheerful.

Some of this joy was soon displaced by a feeling of profound depression. Why on earth had I behaved in such a stupid way? It was past belief.

I finally caught a tram and had the top deck to myself all the way to Ladywood Park, staring out into the darkness as we rattled along the track through the playing fields, alone with my thoughts.

I took them to Jake, naturally. Couldn't possibly have gone to bed without seeing him. I told him everything as he brewed the tea, and he took it all very calmly indeed.

"But I don't really see what's worrying you, old sport," he said. "She's seeing you again, isn't she?"

"But why did I behave like that?" I said. "Like some mad rapist on the loose."

"A slight exaggeration." He started to fill his pipe, a new affectation. "You've got to learn not to let your frustration get the upper hand. No point going at it like a bull at a gate. Females are like rare china. They need delicate handling. They don't like being mauled."

He said a few more things which I can't recall and finally gave me a book on how to achieve marital bliss, which he assured me I would find most enlightening, and threw me out.

When I got home, I sat in the kitchen with another pot of tea and read the book through, or rather the relevant sections. It was obvious that I had a great deal to learn, particularly about the female of the species and how to switch her on.

When I went up to my room, I sat by the open window staring out at the rain lancing through the lamplight, smoking and thinking decidedly erotic thoughts, which did me no good at all. Sleep was also impossible so I did what I always did at such moments, got out my foolscap pads and favorite pen and got down to some hard writing.

I had put away my previous effort, and was now into the second chapter of a novel of life in occupied Germany as a national serviceman. As always when the words took control, everything faded, even Helen.

Helen

• • •

But I couldn't write all the time, and she filled my thoughts obsessively during the following two days. The desire for her became a kind of constant itch that simply wouldn't go away.

I was one of the first inside the Trocadero when it opened at seven and waited impatiently at a point on the balcony where I could see everything at the right end of the hall. It was even quieter than on Tuesday, and everything had a curiously muted air. From seven-thirty to eight was a species of living hell, a slow realization that she wasn't coming. By eight-fifteen I was in a state of abject misery and capable, I think, of leaping over the rail to the floor below.

I went to the counter and got a coffee, and as I turned, she hurried along the balcony toward me, still wearing her coat, her handbag over her shoulder. Her face was flushed and she was slightly breathless, as if she had been running.

"I'm sorry," she said. "I couldn't get away any earlier." And then, by way of further explanation, "My mother can be a little difficult at times."

I just stood there staring at her, unable to believe she was really there. "I didn't think you were coming," I whispered, and then the cup started to rattle in the saucer I was holding.

She moved very close and put an arm around my neck, her face against my shoulder. I could feel her heart beating, or was it mine? It didn't really matter. I put the cup and saucer down on the table and walked her to the cloakroom, where I got my trench coat, and we left.

. . .

About a quarter of a mile along a side road near the Trocadero was a small wood beside a stream. Known as Priory Grange, it was run by the city parks department and was a favorite haunt of courting couples.

I kissed her once in the entrance before moving inside, and we followed a path through the dark trees, arms entwined about each other, and finally emerged by a gray stone wall at the top of a rise on the edge of a small hill.

The moon was about three-quarters full, the wind stirred the grass gently, perfumed with pine from the trees below. There was a hollow on the other side of some rhododendron bushes that was completely secluded. We paused there to kiss again.

"Put your coat on the ground," she whispered. "We'll sit down."

I had been holding myself in tightly, but the moment I got down beside her I cracked, pushing her back against the ground, crushing her to me.

"Gently, darling, gently," she said and stroked my face with one hand. "There's no need to be rough. No need at all."

She looked lovely, her face pale in the moonlight. It could not be happening, any of it, I told myself, as she drew me down. The moment I entered her, the tension of the past few days exploded, Ava all over again.

"I'm sorry," I said.

"What for?" She kissed me firmly on the mouth. "It sometimes happens that way. There's nothing wrong. You'll soon learn."

There was kindness in her voice and genuine concern. I'd heard the phrase "Wife, mistress and mother." Now, for the first time, I sensed just what lay behind it.

She seemed the most wonderful human being in the whole world to me then as we lay there in the moonlight. After a while, in the middle of one particularly passionate kiss, she rolled over on her back again, taking me with her.

This time it was different, a perfect matching. I murmured foolish, impossible things in her ear between the kisses, and then her hands tightened behind my back and her entire body shook with a sudden explosion that took me with her.

After a while she sat up and arranged her clothing, then she put a hand to my face in that inimitable gesture of hers. "Perfect."

I asked her again for a date, but she shook her head. "I'm sorry, Oliver. It just isn't possible at the moment. I can manage Tuesday night again at the Trocadero. I'll try not to be late."

I had to be content, but then, in the state I was in, I would have accepted anything, and we went back down through the trees and along the road, our footsteps echoing from the pavement.

● ● ●

I once read somewhere of a theory that each man can expect only a certain measured amount of happiness in this life and no more. If that be true, then God help me, for I must have used up an inordinate amount of my own ration during the period that followed.

Other things were happening to me, of course.

Important things. These were the first two months of my brief career as a schoolteacher, for example, but life, on looking back, seemed all Helen.

It was an autumnal affair. Sharp, crisp evenings, a hint of woodsmoke in the air, fog crouching at the ends of the streets. Life, for a while, became the Trocadero and Helen, three times a week, for after that first week, she had started to meet me there on Fridays also. Strange, but she would never go anywhere else, not even to the cinema, and things followed a very definite routine. We usually danced until nine o'clock. This was followed by a couple of hours in the field above Priory Grange wood. Then, at eleven, I would walk her to the tram.

The weather must have gone through a reasonably dry spell because, unless memory plays me false, we were not often rained out. We made love constantly and with increasing expertise on my part for, as the old saying goes, practice makes perfect.

But very quickly she came to mean more to me than the mere physical side of things. She was Helen. The scent of pines in the darkness, the wind through the grass, kindness, concern, love. Yes, she loved me. I was convinced of that and took a childish delight in my newfound ability to give her so much pleasure. And the truth was that I loved her as well.

I blossomed, became a completely different person. There was a new assurance. Even Jake commented on that. Aunt Alice, noticing my happiness, told me that Jupiter was moving through a very fortunate phase for me.

But others noticed the difference. Girls at the Trocadero. Sometimes I'd have the odd dance or two while waiting for Helen, and my attitude now was completely different. Lots of easy conversation and plenty of mild flirtation. I could have been away with any number of girls because I had quite simply changed, by some mysterious alchemy, into a man who had been places and done things, or something of the sort.

· · ·

But everything has to come to an end sometime. A sad fact, but quite inescapable for all that. On the other hand, life does have its compensations, and the lesser gods have a habit of at least allowing us to sample the quintessence of a thing before taking it away from us completely.

As I have said elsewhere, Uncle Herbert seldom left the house, but a bad attack of bronchitis gave him a troublesome cough, something he could not afford, having been gassed at Ypres. Aunt Alice, in spite of her more eccentric activities, had never weakened in her concern for him and, with the doctor's blessing, took him off to Scarborough in a rented car for some sea air.

I was left alone to fend for myself and didn't do too badly, in spite of rationing. I tried some tinned whale meat one night, a delicacy new on the British market, large quantities having been imported earlier that year to alleviate the meat shortage. The taste of the stuff put me on the side of the whale conservationists for life, and I spent the rest of the week on a diet of beans and chips augmented by school dinners and the odd meal provided by Jake's mother.

There were other possibilities in having the

house to myself, and I raised the matter with Helen when I met her at the Trocadero on Tuesday. I suggested that we spend Thursday evening indoors. The possibilities seemed endless, and I felt sure she would agree, as it was wet that week.

But she wouldn't hear of it, and I accepted with as good a grace as I could muster for I'd experienced on too many occasions the futility of arguing once she had made up her mind.

On Thursday night it was pouring down, a steady, drenching rain that kept us inside the Trocadero till closing time. When I walked her to the tram stop, we sheltered in a shop doorway as we waited.

As the tram came, she turned to kiss me and said, "I'll be earlier tomorrow, Oliver. Seven o'clock. Wait for me outside, will you?"

She was gone before I could take it further, and I crossed to my own tram stop vaguely disturbed; in all the time I had known her she had always met me inside the Trocadero. But all was revealed when I arrived on the following evening some five minutes late. She was already waiting for me, a small leather vanity bag in one hand.

I kissed her briefly on the cheek. "What's all this then?"

For the first time since I had known her she seemed shy and uncertain of herself. "I'm staying the night with you."

I took a deep breath. "You mean the whole night?"

She nodded. "Is that all right?"

Which only goes to prove that even the best of women are capable, on occasion, of asking the most stupid questions imaginable.

Helen

• • •

She made an excellent supper for us. We sat in the parlor and played Monopoly, and she tried a little Chopin on Aunt Alice's old square Schiedmayer piano, a relic of empire, if you like, for inside it said in faded gold lettering, "Specially Made for the Climate of India."

Later we went up to the turret room together. I used the bathroom first and was in bed when she came in, which meant that I could savor that most intimate of all experiences, a beautiful woman undressing for bed.

I had never seen her naked before. It was a new experience, and not just sexual. More than that, much more. Something quite profound that touched the very heart of things. When she came over to the bed, she sat on the edge and ruffled her fingers through my hair. Beyond, in the moonlight, I could see our reflection in the wardrobe mirror, and beyond that, in an infinity of mirrors. Some trick of the light, I supposed, yet it gave me an uneasy feeling.

• • •

We had breakfast and I saw her to the tram by eight-thirty the following morning. She had told her mother she was staying the night with a girlfriend after attending somebody's annual dance in Bradford and had promised to catch an early train home.

I had never seen her look prettier. She kissed me briefly as the tram rattled down the hill and ground to a halt. The conductor reached for her arm as she stepped onto the platform.

"Tuesday," she called as the tram pulled away.

But I was to see her again before that. Early on Sunday evening Jake had come around to look for me. His mother's brother, a prosperous wool merchant, was staying with them for the weekend and had offered him the loan of his car for the evening, a prewar Riley saloon.

Jake suggested a drink in the country at a Wharfedale pub he'd often talked about, but which I had never visited. I agreed; time and chance again, I suppose.

Wharfedale was a pleasant village by the river, and the pub at that time still retained a lot of its old-world charm. It was fairly busy, mostly locals, but there were at least half a dozen cars drawn up outside when we arrived.

Sitting in the window seat, I was halfway through my first pint, and Jake had gone to prise some decent cigarettes out of the landlord. I watched idly as a car drew up outside, another prewar model, but a Bentley for all that.

There were two men in the front seats, two women in the rear, a happy foursome, all good friends to judge by the laughter. Helen was the first one out. She stood there waiting for the others, nicely turned out in a light-green coat with matching dress.

The man who took her arm had graying hair and looked fifty. Well-dressed, prosperous. Some sort of businessman perhaps. They passed so close to the open window that I could have reached out to touch them. Close enough for me to see the wedding ring on her left hand. There was a kind of inevitability to it for there was nowhere to run. I sat there, waiting. The door opened and in they came.

I heard the gray-haired man, presumably her husband, say, "And what about you, darling?"

She asked for a sherry and he went to the bar, and in the same instant she saw me. Her heart may have missed a beat, but certainly she gave no sign, could not afford to, for the other man had given her a cigarette and was now proffering a light.

So many things made sense now. What, precisely, were the circumstances which had forced her out three nights a week to seek whatever it was she needed elsewhere, I would never know. Certainly her husband, if such he was, seemed pleasant enough, and she smiled with real affection when he handed her the drink.

Jake returned with the cigarettes. I stood up and emptied my glass. "Let's try somewhere else. This is getting too busy."

He nodded, swallowed the rest of his beer and led the way out. I paused at the door and glanced back for the last time. There would be no more Tuesday nights at the Trocadero, I knew that.

For a moment, while the others had their heads together, that mask of hers slipped, a kind of mute appeal on her face, the hand with the wedding ring pushed forward across the table.

I smiled once with all the reassurance that I could muster. I think she understood. I hope so, for I owed her so much. It may have been my imagination, but I fancied a kind of relief on her face as I turned away.

I never set eyes on her again.

4 IMOGENE

A jut with her bum would stir an anchoret.
—William Congreve

It was years before the term "Blackboard Jungle" became notorious. When it did, I always felt that I knew exactly what they were talking about, having served at Khyber Street.

It was a depressing business from that first Monday morning. A friend of Jake's, noticing us waiting for a tram at the park gates, gave us a lift into town in his car. He dropped me about a quarter of a mile from the school but at a point where I had to approach it from a different direction than was to become normal.

I picked my way through an area which had been badly hit by bombing in the war, an undulating brickfield with the odd row of houses still standing here and there. Somewhere in the distance was the sound of the sea breaking on the shore, an impossibility, surely. When I reached the edge of the brickfield, the ground dropped steeply into a carpet of narrow streets, terrace houses, the air thick with morning smoke, and the source of that noise became plain. It was the roar from Khyber Street.

The yard, small as it was, was divided by a brick wall topped by wicked rusting spikes—girls on one side, boys on the other, for rape and worse were expected at an early age. The boys' yard seemed crammed to bursting point. Certainly I had to use physical force to get to the entrance, and the noise was unbelievable. It was more like a mob howling at some palace gate than anything else. An unnerving experience.

Varley, the ginger-haired boy from the day of the interview, and his bovine friend, whose name, as I learned later, was Hatch, lounged against the door, kicking out at any smaller fry who came anywhere near. Prepared for trouble, I girded my loins to meet it. In fact, Varley did everything but touch his forelock, opening the door for me with scrupulous politeness.

"Mornin', sir!" he said gruffly. "Hope you like it here, sir."

"Why, thank you," I told him and went inside, considerably moved by this evidence of a sunnier side to his nature. It only went to prove, of course, that most human beings were essentially decent under the skin. The door to the woodwork room was open, and my friend in the brown coverall was standing at one of the benches lighting a pipe.

"You didn't think better on it," he called.

I moved into the room. It was smaller than I had imagined. Ten ancient wooden benches, tools in racks along the walls, brown-painted cupboards and, even here, the statutory blackboard on the wall behind the desk.

"Oliver Shaw," I said and held out my hand.

"Walter Oldroyd." He grinned. "Intelligence, wasn't it? I was in the paratroops myself. Comes in useful round here at times."

He started to lay tools out neatly on the bench, which I immediately took to be some kind of dismissal. I could not have been more wrong, for as I was to discover, he was one of the kindest men imaginable—a sort of latter-day Fabian trying to come to terms with a world gone mad.

"I suppose I'd better report in," I said.

"Staff room's top of the second stairs," he told me as I moved to the door. "Brace yourself, lad. It isn't much. I make my own tea, break and dinner. You're welcome any time you feel like it."

He obviously didn't expect a reply, was already busy at one of the cupboards, his back to me, so I went out and climbed the stairs.

The staff room was unbelievable, a small cubbyhole with a window at one end at floor level so that it was necessary to bend down to look out of it. There was a gas ring on a table in one corner and a cubicle of hardboard in the other, which I discovered, to my astonishment, contained a lavatory.

Carter stood by the window drinking tea with two other men, a cigarette dangling from the center of his lips. There was something close to relief on his face when I entered. Perhaps he had imagined I might cry off at the last moment. This was very probably the case, for, as I soon discovered, there was a high rate of staff turnover at Khyber Street. Few people with anything about them stayed longer than a year.

He introduced me to my two colleagues. Mr. Johnson was a tall, cadaverous man in a shabby brown suit, the cuffs of which had been bound with leather. Mr. Slater was a younger man who, rather incongruously for the surroundings, wore a purple blazer and a striped tie, relics of his college days to which he hung on desperately, as a drowning man clutches at a life jacket.

"You've met the deputy, have you?" Carter asked me.

"The deputy?" I asked, bewildered.

"The deputy headmaster. Our Mr. Oldroyd."

I nodded, gaining further insight into the redoubtable Wally's character, for most teachers I ever met would have brandished their status like a headman's ax above my head at the earliest opportunity.

Someone broke wind inside the cubicle, there was a certain amount of movement, the purpose of which one could only guess at, and then the chain was pulled. The aroma which became apparent after that was all-pervading and left a great deal to be desired. The door opened outward, which meant that because of the confined space, a certain amount of jockeying for position was necessary.

"Hurry up, Schwartz, for goodness sake?" Mr. Carter said impatiently.

Poor Schwartz, who had been bullied by someone or other for most of his life. First the Nazis, now Carter. He was small and rather plump, his shoulders permanently hunched, dark eyes peering anxiously from behind an ancient pair of gold-rimmed spectacles.

He wore a neat dark coat, a gray waistcoat with a watch chain, and striped trousers. I wondered wildly whether he was perhaps attending a wedding later in the day, but discovered that these were the only clothes in which he had ever been seen.

This, then, was the staff. Six of us, including the headmaster, to control two hundred and forty-one boys. As Mr. Carter never taught, it gave us a ratio of forty-eight boys to each teacher, but luckily the incredibly high absenteeism kept this down to more manageable figures.

I was to pass the first week gaining experience by spending my time with each member of the staff in rotation, which seemed a sensible enough idea, as it was reasonable to assume that I could actually learn from them, although time was to prove otherwise.

Morning assembly was an interesting experience. The boys were marched in class by class, and they occupied one side of the hall. Only when they were in position were the girls allowed in from the other side, shepherded by five assorted ladies who even at that distance seemed no more prepossessing than my own colleagues.

There was a considerable amount of noise and laughter to an extent that astonished me, and I got the distinct impression that the older boys were actually calling out to the older girls, many of whom seemed disconcertingly mature for their age.

Mr. Carter walked in briskly, got up on a wooden box behind the lectern and hammered on it with a ruler. "I will not tolerate this disgusting noise!" he screamed.

There was immediate silence and they all waited, presumably as fascinated by his performance as I was. "Hymn two hundred and thirty-three," he went on.

Mr. Schwartz, who had been waiting at the piano, struck out boldly and everyone launched into "All Things Bright and Beautiful."

There was nothing beautiful about it, and when it was finished, there was considerable shuffling. Mr. Carter waited grimly, and gradually all heads were bowed. He kept his own eyes open, hands clasped before him, and commenced to pray loudly, punctuating every few lines with that awful graveyard cough of his.

"Oh, God," he intoned. "Make us like Thee in every way. Teach us how to go forth into the world in the image of Thine only begotten son, Christ Jesus, our only burden love and Christian charity, all men our brother. . . ."

At this point he descended from the box with incredible speed, scattering boys like ninepins. Presumably they were used to these forays because there was not the instant panic I would have imagined.

I saw his hands rising and falling, and finally the crowd parted and a boy stumbled forth, arms raised to protect his head. A smallish boy, I noted. In fact, in all the time I was on his staff I never knew Carter to assault any of the older boys in a similar manner, although on occasion he would simulate such an attack with much shouting and dramatic posturing. He cuffed the boy all the way to the door and tossed him out into the corridor, then returned to the lectern and glared at the entire assembly.

"That lout." He ground his teeth together. "That filthy beast out there"—here he pointed, hand shaking—"is not fit for decent company."

Everyone there seemed as mystified as I was myself. I never did find out what the wretched boy was supposed to have done. My own theory after seeing several such incidents over a period of time, was that it was all quite simply a ploy on Carter's part. He liked, I think, to imagine himself a holy terror. Such actions were deliberately calculated to enhance his image.

The rest of the staff seemed unconcerned enough except Wally Oldroyd, and there was a kind of contempt on his face as Carter brushed past him on the way out.

• • •

It seems to me that one of the deficiencies of the teaching profession is its insistence that all its members are dedicated intellectuals who have voluntarily turned their backs on the world of industry and commerce, where they would undoubtedly have made their fortunes, to devote themselves to the service of youth.

I never met anyone like that at Khyber Street other than Wally Oldroyd, who did a solid professional job. The rest were shabby little men who would have been inadequate at anything they put their hand to. Khyber Street was their final resting place, the end of the line. There was simply nowhere else to go, which didn't help their charges, most of whom were the products of the kind of home with which Charles Dickens would have been perfectly familiar. It was all very sad.

I felt sorry most of all for Mr. Schwartz, who was pathetically grateful for the chance to have a job—a job of any kind. He had been a teacher of music in a Munich conservatory for many years, but that was before the concentration camps. At Khyber Street he took each class for singing once a week, which meant that for most of the time he was expected to teach English and general subjects.

Considering that he spoke a kind of pidgin English, the effect can be imagined. He survived only because he had Class One, the youngest boys in the school. Anyone older and he would have been trampled into the floorboards. I spent a full day with him and learned nothing except how to fill the register, enter up milk bottle returns, school dinners and the like.

My visit with Johnson must have lasted for a similar period, but lives in my memory by reason of one incident only. When I accompanied him into Class Three, pandemonium reigned. Two or three boys struggled on the floor, there was a card game going on in the corner, everyone else seemed to be reading comics.

Johnson, who I learned later had only a year to go to retirement, showed not the slightest concern. He opened the register, glanced briefly about the room, then filled it in as prescribed in an exquisite scarlet and blue copperplate which must have endeared him to the headmaster's heart, for Mr. Carter was keen on registers.

When this task was accomplished, he opened his briefcase, produced a sheet of sums, turned his back on the class and, completely disregarding the din, proceeded to copy them on the blackboard in the same neat copperplate. When he was finished, he dusted his hands, sat down behind the desk and took out a newspaper.

No one appeared to take the slightest notice. "Is there anything you'd like me to do?" I asked, almost shouting because of the din.

He made no reply. I touched him on the arm. He glanced around inquiringly, then took a hearing aid on its wire from his breast pocket and shoved it into his ear. "Anything I can do for you, old man?" he asked.

But there was nothing. Nothing anyone could do, or so I was beginning to imagine.

•   •   •

Varley was in the top class and was supposed to be leaving school the following Easter. The class teacher was Slater, the young man of the purple blazer and striped tie.

The morning I joined him he put on an impressive display of shouting that would not have disgraced Mr. Carter at his worst. On no less than three occasions before break, he caned boys soundly, two blows on each hand. I was puzzled. In each case, the punishment followed general insolence from

Varley and his cronies, yet the individuals chosen seemed to me to be the smallest or at least the most inoffensive in the class.

He did a considerable amount of reading to them, mostly cheap thrillers or adventure stories and allowed them at least an hour's private study each day during which they could read what they wanted, and usually did.

All this time was noted on his syllabus as being devoted to "A general introduction to English literature by which the child would be enabled to enlarge his world by exploring for himself interesting themes in contemporary fiction."

This and similar twaddle concerning other lessons was neatly typed out and ready for inspection at any time. I never once saw him actually teach anybody anything or even try.

During the time I was with him, he left me on my own for considerable periods. At first they weren't too bad. I was treated with a sort of gruff respect that was vaguely flattering. Varley and Hatch had seen me in uniform on the first day. It was known I had been in the army, and I was asked to recount my experiences.

I was surprised at what an interesting time I'd had when I went over my two years of serving king and country. The only trouble was that whenever I actually tried to teach I was in immediate trouble.

I had prepared several lessons, some English and history particularly, trying to link them together. No one took the slightest notice and one day I discovered a card game in one corner and dominoes in the other—a humiliating echo of Johnson's situation.

When I spoke to Slater about this he shrugged. "They're leaving at Easter, old man. Couldn't care less, and you can't really blame 'em."

All right, so I had already discovered beyond any shadow of a doubt that I didn't have any vocation, but at least I did have some sort of compulsion to earn my money.

I raised the problem with Wally next time we had tea together, for I had taken him up on his original offer, his workshop being infinitely preferable to the staff room with its cubicle toilet. I put the matter as delicately as possible, for Wally was, after all, deputy headmaster. He let me talk, filling his pipe at the same time.

"Am I expecting too much?" I asked him finally.

"You are, as far as this place is concerned," he said. "Forget all that fancy talk, lad. In a school like this we're keeping them off the streets and out of everybody's way, and in large numbers. That's what society pays us for. We're a custodial institution."

"But surely we can do better than that?"

"You have to do the best with what you've got, Oliver. Carter doesn't want any trouble, so don't start any because he won't back you up. That's the main reason discipline stinks here. Trying to teach the way you want is a waste of time. Too many in the class anyway. Keep their heads down with plenty of written work. 'Turn to page seventy-three and do the next twenty sums' are probably the finest words in the English language from the teacher's point of view."

"And, Oliver," he called as I moved to the door, "remember one thing. The welfare of the teacher is of paramount importance at all times."

• • •

Slater fractured his right leg in a rugby game the following Saturday. On Monday morning, Mr. Carter announced that I would take over the top class until he was fit to return.

It was a ridiculous decision in view of my lack of experience but I took up the challenge bravely, remembering Wally's advice, sorted through the stock cupboard and made certain that everyone had a copy of the relevant textbook in each subject and had signed for it. I was now able to tell the boys to turn to any page in the book in any subject at the drop of a hat and start writing.

They didn't like it, and a kind of desperate guerrilla warfare broke out. I managed to stem the flow of disappearing books by informing them, quite untruthfully, that any not available the following day would have to be paid for. I added darkly, that as they were city property, the police would call in person at their homes for the money.

Which took care of that problem. Things took a nastier turn after that. Dog dirt in a neatly wrapped parcel which I found on my desk one day. Even worse, human excrement in a piece of newspaper was thrown at the blackboard when I had my back turned, narrowly missing me.

I had no means of knowing the culprit, although Varley and Hatch seemed the obvious choices. There didn't appear to be much I could do, for any kind of physical violence was out. As a probationer, I was not entitled to use corporal punishment during my first year.

84

I made Varley and Hatch clean up the mess, then announced that the entire class would have to stay in at four o'clock. This didn't go well as most of them had paper routes or jobs of one sort or another after school.

At afternoon break, Mr. Carter sought me out and drew me into the privacy of his office. "I understand you intend to keep your class in after school?"

"That's right," I said. "Who told you?"

He didn't like that. "I make it my business to know what's going on in my own school, Mr. Shaw. Frankly, I think you're quite mistaken in this matter. I don't think we've any right to their time after four o'clock."

"Good God, man," I said, "have you any idea what they did?"

"To impose a penalty on the whole class because of something which arises out of your own lax discipline is something I will not tolerate, Mr. Shaw."

He was seized by a paroxysm of coughing, and I turned and walked out. Why I didn't get my coat and keep on going I'll never know. I was seeing Helen that night, which was something to look forward to, but I think it was more fundamental. I simply couldn't stand the thought of being beaten by a crew like that, and I was including Carter and his band of merry men as well as the boys.

• • •

My authority had been completely undermined and it showed. For the rest of the week discipline in the class was terrible, and there were times when I gave up and let it all wash over me, emulating Johnson by sitting at the desk with my hands over my ears reading the newspaper, while they did exactly as they pleased.

Things came to a head, in a sense, on the following Monday morning when I arrived at the class a few minutes late owing to a message, which proved to have no foundation in fact, that Carter wanted me. I should have been warned by the unnatural stillness as I approached the room. When I opened the door it fell down.

There was a chorus of shocked gasps as I stepped across the door, mock horror on every face. "What have you done, sir?" Varley inquired piously.

I was as close to committing murder as I have ever been, but did not descend on him at once for the simple reason that rage rooted me to the spot. As it happened, matters were taken out of my hands.

"What on earth is going on here?" someone demanded sharply and I turned and set eyes on Imogene for the first time.

· · ·

I had heard of her, of course, in the men's staff room —the glamorous Imogene who took girls for Games and Cookery, a mixture not quite as bizarre as it sounded. She had been on some course or other at the local teaching college for a couple of weeks, which explained why I'd never met her.

But no description could possibly have done justice to the reality of her. She was every man's fantasy. A creature out of the pages of some film magazine. Masses of red-gold hair, slanting green eyes, a mouth half a smile wide. And the body! What could one possibly say about that except that the lesser gods had been more than generous with her.

She wore tennis shoes and short white socks, green shorts and a sports shirt. A whistle, suspended from a ribbon around her neck, nestled between two of the most magnificent breasts I've ever seen in my life.

"What on earth's going on?" she demanded.

Every boy in the room gazed at her, their expressions varying from frank admiration to naked lust.

"Mr. Shaw knocked down the door, miss," Varley said. "Didn't he, lads?"

Here he appealed to the class, which responded dutifully. He turned, grinning, his fingers hooked into his belt of badges.

"Don't play the fool with me," Imogene said cheerfully and held out her hand. "Where are they?"

"Where's what, miss?"

"The screws. The screwdriver."

He looked around the room in apparent bewilderment, then shrugged helplessly. "It were 'im, Miss. Mr. Shaw . . ."

He got no further. She slapped him across the face, a solid, openhanded punch with all her weight behind it that sent him staggering back against a cupboard. As he rebounded, she gave him a dose of the same across the left cheek.

The silence in the room was absolute. Varley glared wildly about him. "Don't try my patience, boy," she said in a bored voice, and hit him again. "Now, where are they?"

He lurched to one of the book cupboards, fumbled about in the bottom and produced a handful of screws and a screwdriver. He put them down on the desk with shaking hands.

"That's a good boy," she said in the same cool, bored voice. "Now you and your little friends can get that door back where it was, can't you?"

Varley stared at the floor sullenly. She took a short step toward him and he jumped out of the way. "All right, miss," he said.

She turned to me. "I see your hand is bleeding, Mr. Shaw. There's a first-aid kit in the hall. If you'd like to come through I'll fix it for you. I'm taking a class in there."

She walked out, poetry in motion. I turned to the class and saw that every lad was gazing after her in a kind of blissful adoration. But then, if ever a woman was the great earth mother of all men, it was Imogene.

"Right, thanks," I said gruffly and followed her out.

A class of twelve-year-old girls played netball in vests and knickers as they waited for her. She turned from the first-aid box, a bandage in one hand, as I joined her.

"This will have to do for the time being," she said. "If you come down to my room at break I'll put a plaster on it for you."

It wasn't much of a cut but there was a fair amount of blood. When her fingers touched me lightly, my stomach went hollow.

I thanked her and went back to the classroom in some confusion. Varley, Hatch and a couple of other boys were busy at the door. The rest of the class were strangely silent, aware, I suppose of Imogene out in the hall within hearing distance.

I told them to get out their geography books and copy the map on page seventy-three, aware of Varley's bright malevolent eyes switching constantly my way. He muttered something to Hatch, I couldn't hear what, and there was a general snigger among the group at the door.

Hatch glanced toward me furtively, then suddenly he cocked a leg to one side and broke wind. Poor wretch—like Dirty George, it was his only accomplishment.

I cracked completely. I opened the lid of the old-fashioned desk and grabbed Slater's cane. I was across the room and had Hatch by the scruff of his neck and over the nearest desk before he knew what was happening. I slashed him good and hard three or four times across the backside, then threw him into the seat behind his desk, howling his head off.

A shocked voice said from the doorway behind me, "Good heavens, Mr. Shaw, what is the meaning of this?"

By now the door itself was in position. I pointed sternly, and Varley and the others sat down hurriedly and got on with their work.

"Mr. Shaw, I asked you a question," Carter demanded.

"There's your answer." I waved the cane at the class. "They're working, for once. They're working because I used this. Brute force, Mr. Carter. As my old aunty would say, it's enough to make you weep."

"It is strictly against regulations for a probationary teacher to . . ."

I pushed him into the corridor and closed the

door behind me. "All right, report me," I said. "Get me the sack. I couldn't care less. It would suit me just fine to walk out of this place right now."

But it wouldn't have suited him, not by a long chalk for he hadn't the slightest hope of replacing me at that time of the year. To get me at all had been a small miracle in the first place.

He tried to look dignified. "There's no need for that tone, young man. Another thing. I would remind you that you signed a contract—a contract to run to the end of term. As for your insolence, you'll hear from me later."

But I didn't, not a word, and from then on he left me severely alone.

• • •

Imogene had a small office at one end of the cookery room. When I knocked on the door she asked who it was. I told her, and a bolt was withdrawn and the door opened.

I went in and found her in the middle of dressing. She was in the process of fastening her bra at the back, and she wore a wrapover skirt in brown jersey which accentuated the splendid curves of her hips.

"I'll only be a moment," she said. "I've just made some tea, if you'd like to pour it."

I filled two cups and stirred in condensed milk, aware of the rustle of silk behind me as she pulled on her blouse. When I turned, I was disconcerted to find her with the skirt hitched up, adjusting a garter. I had a brief, heart-stopping glimpse of flesh above the tan nylon stocking, and then she dropped the skirt and pulled on her shoes.

I sat down and she unwound the bandage. I said, "I'd like to thank you."

"For clobbering that little rat?" She shrugged. "It's the only way to handle them, you know. They'll stamp you into the ground if you let them."

"It isn't their fault."

"I know," she said. "Environment, heredity. You name it, they've got it, from congenital syphilis to nits. I'm afraid I'm only interested in the situation as I find it, not the reasons behind it."

Which made sense. One had to survive in that hellhole after all. She stood with one of her legs between my knees, the scent of her filled my nostrils so that I turned dizzy, and her breasts, which in that position were right in front of my eyes, seemed to grow larger by the second.

I tried to think of Helen and failed miserably as Imogene swabbed the cut, her leg nudging my hand. I pressed slightly as if by accident. She did not move away. My stomach churning, I slipped the hand just under the hem of her dress. She moved closer, a slight frown on her face, and reached for a plaster. I took a deep breath and slid the hand up that long nylon flank.

She frowned again, concentrating as she fixed the plaster. "There, that's better." She looked down at me and patted my face. "You're all the same, you men. God's gift to women in your own imagination." She kissed me unexpectedly and moved across to the table to the first-aid kit. "I could do a better job on myself with my middle finger than the lot of you put together."

Which was about as dampening a remark as I had

ever heard in that area. I stood up and she smiled. "Oh, poor Oliver. It is Oliver, isn't it? Have I upset him? Tell you what, I'll let you take me for a drink tonight if you like."

"I'm sorry," I said. "I've got a date."

"And you so active with your hands. Shame on you." She smiled beautifully and ran the tip of her tongue between her teeth. "Some other time, perhaps? When the great romance is over."

I retreated in confusion. I loved Helen and a man in love shouldn't feel this kind of physical attraction for another woman, or so I told myself.

• • •

Life at school settled into an uneasy kind of guerrilla warfare. I made the boys work, therefore I was hated. I was rocking what had been a pretty comfortable boat. But I had reached the state where I couldn't care less, even about the very real hatred that Varley and his friends obviously felt for me. I had my writing to keep me sane, with its hope of something better than this, and I had Helen.

And then, suddenly, Helen was gone. For a week or two I was in a state of abject misery that even kept me from the Trocadero. I was like the "before" man in an ad for some wonder tonic. Listless, no energy, lacking interest in life.

Things started to slide in the class again. It became noisier; the hostility, barely veiled at the best of times, became more open.

One afternoon just before the Christmas holidays, I cut my finger wrestling with a jammed door on one of my stock cupboards and was reminded of Imogene. It was as good an excuse as any. I wrapped a handkerchief around the finger and went in search of her. She was taking some girls for netball in the yard. I stood at the door watching the game for a while, admiring the way Imogene's breasts tightened against her shirt when she demonstrated how to throw the ball.

"Hello, stranger, looking for me?" she said as she hurried in, followed by the girls, at the end of the game. I held up my finger and she smiled. "What does that need? Sticking plaster or tea and sympathy?"

I followed her into her office and sat down. She got the first-aid kit and unwrapped the handkerchief. "Watching the girl's knickers again, Oliver?"

"Only one girl's knickers I was watching out there," I said boldly.

She stared down at me, the slanting green eyes changing color constantly. And then she smiled. "All right, Oliver. If you want it you can have it."

"When?" I said.

"Why, now, of course. We've got the rest of break, haven't we?"

She went to the door and shot the bolt, then pulled one of the gym mats out of the corner and unrolled it. I was absolutely petrified. I stood staring at her as she unhooked her shorts and pulled them off.

"Have you got anything with you?" she demanded. I shook my head and she reached for her handbag and produced a contraceptive. "Service with a smile, that's us. Now hurry up, there's a lovely boy. We've only got ten minutes."

In the circumstances, I couldn't be expected to give of my best, was not really able to savor to the full the delights she had to offer. I worked away manfully, covering her with kisses as I warmed to my work.

At one point, gazing up beyond my shoulder, she said calmly, "That bloody ceiling's going to fall in one of these days. I really must have a word with old Carter about it"—a remark which was hardly calculated to help one give of one's best. As I finished, she kissed me fiercely and started to stimulate herself quite vigorously with the middle finger of her right hand, reaching a climax with remarkable speed.

"Oh, that was lovely." She gave a great shuddering sigh and smiled up at me. "Don't be downhearted, Oliver. You might bring me off yet, though you'll be the first bloke to manage it if you do."

I was too astonished to reply. In the middle distance the bell started to ring. "Ah, well, back to the salt mines."

She stood up and wriggled into her shorts, the most maddeningly attractive woman I had ever known and the most unreachable.

"Of course I am rather taking it for granted that you do want more."

She moved very close and peered into my eyes as if she was trying to see what was going on inside, and then she smiled. "I wonder what the top class would think if they knew what we've been doing."

I turned and ran as if all the devils in hell were at my heels.

• • •

Of course, it was easily explained in psychological terms. She had this enormous power over men and enjoyed taking advantage of it, and in a sense the enjoyment was enhanced because of her own invulnerability. Because none of them could actually get through to her.

I took the whole problem to Jake, who didn't seem to find it in any way surprising. "I don't know what you're grumbling about," he said. "They're all different, that's what makes them so bloody marvelous. Variety, after all, is the spice of life."

"It's all right for you to talk," I said, "but it's damn frustrating, I can tell you, working away like a bloody great steam hammer with no apparent result."

"That's the trouble with male ego, hell-bent on orgasm."

It was a fine, fresh evening, the first hint of a winter chill in the air, the moon caught in the branches of the trees on the far side of the park. Jake leaned on the sill of the open window and inhaled deeply with obvious pleasure.

"Come on," I said impatiently. "What do I do?"

" 'She, while her lover pants upon her breast, can mark the figures on an Indian chest.' " He turned, grinning. "Alexander Pope. I think he summed the whole thing up admirably."

"And what's that supposed to mean?" I demanded.

"It seems you either like it or lump it." Another firm old Yorkshire saying. "On the other hand, you can always look elsewhere. In that case, be sure to leave her address."

But that, of course, was the last thing I intended to do.

· · ·

The following Tuesday I persuaded Imogene to go to the Trocadero with me. She looked absolutely superb in a dark-red dress of some kind of silk material, belted tightly at the waist, with a long, flowing multipleated skirt that swirled out in great undulating circles on the turns in the quicksteps.

By far the best-looking girl in the room, she attracted considerable attention. In the general excuse-me dances, I lost her on several occasions, which hardly pleased me. On the other hand, one had to accept with as good a grace as possible.

When she returned after one such dance, she kissed me carelessly on the cheek and slipped a hand through my arm. "I've had enough of this place, Oliver. Where can we go now?"

I was surprised, for it was only nine o'clock. "Are you sure?"

She nodded. "I've never really cared for dancing. A little goes a long way with me."

It was cold outside, but not too cold, a touch of frost in the air and Christmas not much more than a week away. I suggested a drink at The Tall Man, but she shook her head, and we kept on walking in the general direction of Ladywood Park, as she lived no more than a mile from me.

There was a full moon, and the playing fields, touched with hoarfrost, seemed to stretch before us into infinity. On the far left of us my old school looked as if it had been cut out of black paper. Imogene tossed her handbag to me and executed two perfect cartwheels, one after the other. She turned, flinging her arms wide, an ecstatic smile on her face.

"It's a night for adventure, Oliver."

I nodded toward the old Alma Mater. "I know just what you mean. I've had a few over there myself on nights like this."

She glanced across the field at those dark buildings. "School? You've got to be joking."

I shook my head. "No, it's true enough. When I was in my teens a crowd of us used to break in regularly at night. It's easy enough. We never did any damage or anything like that. Just fooled about. Like you say, it was an adventure, creeping about those dark corridors by night. A nice spooky feeling."

She looked across at the school again. "But what did you do in there?"

"Messed about in the gym. Let the ropes down. That sort of thing. And we used to get into the swimming pool and swim in the nude. Great fun until the caretaker surprised us one night."

"Did he catch you?"

I shook my head. "We managed to make a run for it."

Her eyes sparkled in the moonlight and she smiled suddenly. "It sounds marvelous. I can't wait."

She grabbed my hand and pulled me toward the distant school. I said wildly, "What, break in now? You and me? You can't mean it."

She slid an arm about my neck, giving me the full treatment from breast to thigh and kissed me, lips parted. "Just think of swimming naked in the dark in all that gorgeous warm water, Oliver. And I'll be with you. Who knows what delicious, naughty things we might get up to."

97

Which was definitely more than flesh and blood could stand, and when she took my hand in hers again, I went without further protest.

. . .

She insisted on penetrating main block first so I left her waiting impatiently on the steps by the cloakroom entrance at the junior quad and started climbing, just like the old days.

She was right, of course. About the adventure of it, I mean. There was exactly the same excitement the fifteen-year-old had experienced as I climbed the corner of the wall where alternate courses of brick projected, making excellent footholds.

There was nothing particularly dangerous about it and I scrambled over the parapet at the top and paused for breath on the flat roof.

Far, far away in the distance, a tram sailed along the track through the playing fields to the park, brilliantly illuminated, its passengers clearly visible inside. It existed in another world than this, and I stood there, staring out into the dark void, the last man in the world.

"Are you all right, Oliver?"

Imogene's urgent whisper echoed up from the quad, bringing me back to reality. I made for the first floor corridor window we had always used in the past, the one with the broken catch. It opened with a slight protesting creak. I swung a leg over the sill, Raffles to the life, closed the window behind me and went down the stairs.

I opened the cloakroom door and admitted Imogene. She stood very close to me and took my hand, lacing her fingers through mine. "Where's the gym?" she whispered.

We moved along the dark corridor, bands of moonlight filtering across the tall windows, Imogene's high heels clicking slightly. There was a set of changing rooms at the far end. We moved through them, I pushed open a glass door and led the way into the gym.

It had what virtually amounted to a glass wall down one side, and everything was clear in the moonlight. For some reason it gave me a slightly eerie feeling, particularly the ropes which someone had left out. They hung from the ceiling in the dark line, swaying a little as if someone had just been using them.

Imogene was as delighted as a child let loose in a fairground. "How marvelous, how simply marvelous," she cried.

She dropped her coat and handbag to the floor, kicked off her shoes and started to make the rounds of all the equipment, becoming steadily noisier. I followed uneasily, begging her to be quiet, but it did no good. She was thoroughly enjoying herself, and everything else went by the board.

She was a superb gymnast. She did various tricks of one kind or another, all pretty spectacular considering she wasn't dressed for them, and at one point did a perfect handstand in the rings six feet above the ground, her skirt down around her head.

Finally she climbed one of the ropes and was poised up there in the shadows in the very roof of the gym, where I could hardly see her.

"Oliver!" she called. "Remember the first time

you discovered it could be rather pleasant to slide down one of these things?"

She seemed to float out of the shadows into the moonlight as I looked up, the pleated skirt of her dress ballooning out, long, lovely legs, thighs white above the dark stockings in the pale light. She was like some strange flower descending.

I opened my arms and she drifted into them. I kissed her once, and she patted my face and pushed me away firmly.

"Contain yourself, Oliver, there's a good boy. Everything comes to him who waits."

. . .

By now I was so excited that I pretty well threw caution to the winds. When we reached the swimming pool, a single-story building on its own among trees, I took her to the French windows which ran down one side.

"Wait here and I'll let you in in a minute," I told her. "But for God's sake keep your voice down. Old Smith lives in the gate lodge, which isn't all that far away."

There was a small concrete coke bunker with a flat roof against the wall on the other side of the building. Three or four round windows of the kind that pivot in the center to open were easily accessible once I climbed on top. None of their catches ever worked properly in the past and usually a push was all it took to open any one of them.

A moment later and I was standing in the warm darkness between a row of changing cubicles. Was it then or now? For a moment I was fifteen again, and the years meant nothing, a strange feeling. I was brought back to reality by an insistent tapping on one of the French windows.

The moonlight streamed in with a kind of pale luminosity. In the winter months, the boilers were kept going at a high level each night to keep water good and hot for the following day. The whole place was thick with steam so that I could hardly see the diving platform at the far end, and the water was calm as a mill pond.

I moved cautiously around the tiled edge, which was rather slippery, to Imogene, who was standing with her face pressed against the glass. I opened the French window and was careful to bolt it again after she had slipped past me.

She took a deep breath of the muggy, chlorinated air and there was a kind of ecstasy on her face. "Oh, Oliver, I can't wait."

She hurried around the pool to the changing rooms. As I turned to follow, I slipped on the wet tiles and almost went into the water. I took it more cautiously after that, and when I went into the changing room, she'd got rid of her dress and was unfastening her stockings.

"Hurry up, slowcoach," she said as she slipped off her pants and dropped them on the pile on the floor.

I watched her go toward the pool, captivated by that superb body of hers, pale in the moonlight, ethereal, unreal. She disappeared from view. I heard a gentle splash, the sound of swimming.

My heart was beating like a trip-hammer as I undressed quickly and followed her. I stood at the pool's edge, peering about me, unable to see her, which was hardly surprising in all that steam.

"Imogene, where are you?" I whispered.

There was no reply. I sat down on the edge and lowered myself into the water. It was extraordinarily pleasant, more like a warm bath than anything else —and there was that wonderful feeling of freedom that one gets when swimming with nothing on.

I moved toward the deep end, vaguely alarmed. "Imogene!" I called.

She materialized from the mist, poised on top of the high-diving platform, a heart-stopping sight in the moonlight. She dived before I could call out to her, a perfect half-pike, which still made far too much noise for our situation.

She surfaced within a yard of me, laughing, hair clinging to her face. "Isn't it marvelous?"

"You must keep quiet," I hissed. "You're making too much noise."

I suppose I sounded pretty annoyed, but we were in a vulnerable situation, to say the least, if we were discovered. The attitude of authority toward a bunch of teenage boys caught in such circumstances was one thing; a man and a woman, a couple of teachers to boot, were something else again.

"Don't be angry, Oliver." She reached under the water.

My heart was pounding nineteen to the dozen again, and I cupped my hands over her breasts, treading water, for it was eight feet deep at that end.

"You really are the most infuriating girl."

"Take me, Oliver," she said dramatically. "Now, as I am. Naked and unafraid." She smiled. "I've never tried it this way before."

An invitation impossible to deny, and I eagerly moved in at once. Of course, the trouble with most

102

sexual fantasy is that the reality simply can't measure up, and often for the most absurd of reasons.

To the average man the idea of making love to that magnificent creature, drifting languorously in warm, translucent water, must probably sound like the final end to all things. Nirvana achieved.

To start with, I had considerable difficulty in any kind of a union at all below waist level, for in spite of the fact that she floated passively on her back, the currents in the water caused by my approach pushed her away from me.

We went under twice before achieving the necessary connection, and any amount of times after that as I attempted to perform my part. We rolled and twisted in the water, blowing for air like a couple of whales each time we surfaced.

Imogene seemed to find the whole thing enormously funny and she shrieked with laughter, the sound echoing between the walls. I was in no fit state to prevent her, was not even able to help myself. When I went under again, I decided it was for the last time, and threw in my hand. Imogene actually had to life-save me to the side and heave me up out of the water. I lay on my belly, coughing and spluttering, while she pounded me on the back.

"Poor Oliver," she said. "Why didn't you tell me you were such a rotten swimmer?"

A bitter reply formed on my lips, but I never got it out; suddenly, there was a sharp tapping on one of the French windows. I glanced up and to my horror saw Smith peering in.

It was doubtful whether he could actually see us, in spite of the moonlight, what with the mist and the shadows, but he wasn't going to let that stop him.

"Come on out of it!" he shouted. "I know you're in there. You can't get away."

He moved to another window, peering in. To my absolute horror, Imogene dived into the water, swam under the surface to the other side and hauled herself out.

"Imogene!" I called desperately, but I was too late.

She unbolted two of the French windows and flung them open. Immediately steam boiled around her, sucked out by the cold air. God knows what she looked like looming out of the mist, touched by moonlight. A creature from another world.

I saw Smith pause uncertainly beyond her. She flung her arms wide and intoned, "At last! At last! 'Tis I, Astarte. Come for you, my beloved."

Smith gave a hoarse cry, took a hasty step back and fell over a rosebush. He scrambled to his feet, turned and stumbled away into the darkness. There was no time to dry off. I was in the changing room and into my trousers by the time Imogene arrived. She couldn't stop laughing.

"Oh, that poor man," she said. "What will he think?"

"Never mind that now," I urged. "We've got about ninety seconds to get out of here."

Which was probably looking on the dark side a little, but there was no sense in asking for trouble. She pulled on shoes, dress and coat, and everything else went into her handbag. Extraordinary how difficult it was to wriggle into a jacket when soaking wet, but I managed it, buttoned my raincoat to my neck and stuffed underwear, shirt and socks into my pocket. Then we ran for it. Didn't stop until we were halfway across the playing fields, Imogene laughing helplessly all the time.

We reached the tram stop finally and she leaned against me to catch her breath. "Are you all right?" I asked anxiously. "You look as if you've been caught in a monsoon."

She nodded. "Marvelous. What are we doing tomorrow night?"

A tram arrived a few minutes later, which was a good thing because it was getting damned cold. The conductor gave her a hand up, frowned and peered outside as he pressed the bell.

"Hasn't been raining up here, has it?" he asked as he came for the tickets.

"It's been pouring on the other side of the fields," Imogene told him seriously. "Absolutely pouring."

The conductor glanced at her with a touch of alarm, then withdrew silently. I watched him standing out there on the platform, and he put his hand out to feel for rain at least half a dozen times before we reached Ladywood Park.

Imogene hugged my arm. "That was marvelous, Oliver. It really was. What *are* we going to do tomorrow?"

. . .

I think I gave Jake the laugh of his life when I appeared from the night like some fugitive from a chain gang. True to form, he got me a very large whiskey and ran a hot bath, in which I soaked while I told him all.

"What a woman, Oliver," he said. "They must

105

have broken the mold when they made her. My offer still stands. If you don't want her, let me have her."

"The trouble is you never know where you are with her." I sighed heavily. "Do you know what she just told me, cool as you please, before I left her? That she finishes at Khyber Street this week. She won't be back next term."

"Where is she going?" Jake asked.

"Got herself a teaching post in the Bahamas. One of these three-year-contract things."

"The story of my life," he said solemnly and placed a hand on my shoulder. "Make hay while the sun shines, old sport. It will soon be raining again."

But in a way I was rather glad, for I think I knew then that I couldn't stand the pace, though I tried hard enough, God knows.

We were together constantly for the whole fortnight of the Christmas holiday. In fact, I slept with her several times, as she lived on her own in a two-room flat on the far side of the park from me.

I worked myself into a sweat with her on so many occasions that I lost count but never succeeded in achieving any greater success than I had that first time in her little office at school.

I was with her on the final night. On the following day she was to take a train for London, and I was to return to the joys of Khyber Street.

She could be serious enough when she wanted to be and was more subdued than I'd ever known her. I helped her pack, and we went to bed just before midnight and made love, the end result being no different from usual.

I got out of bed and went and sat at the window,

smoking a cigarette. It was raining slightly, and I felt terribly sad and very much at the end of something. After a while, there was a movement behind me, a blanket was slipped around my shoulders and she sat on the window seat beside me.

"That was lovely," she said.

I thought she was just trying to be nice and re-acted accordingly. "Is that a fact?" I said bitterly.

"I'm satisfied, Oliver, you're not," she said. "It's as simple as that. Not everyone is the same. We all have different needs. Why can't you let it go at that?"

She was right. I'd been a stupid, morose idiot, seeing only what I wanted to see, and all because of the worst kind of male pride. I felt a sudden rush of affection for her and put an arm around her shoulder.

"Promise me one thing, Oliver," she said suddenly. "Get out of Khyber Street. It isn't for you."

"What do I do? Write the great novel of the century?"

"Why not?"

I reminded her that my latest effort, a short novel based on my experiences in the army in Berlin, had been rejected by one of the best literary agents in London, although he had been kind enough to say I had promise and he would be willing to handle me.

"Write another book then," she said, which, strangely enough, had been exactly the advice contained in the last paragraph of the agent's letter.

"All right, I'll think about it," I said. "If it comes to anything, I'll dedicate it to you."

"There's my lovely boy." She patted my face. "Now let's get back to bed."

I lay with my arm around her in the darkness for

quite a while, listening to the rain. I thought she was asleep until she said quietly, "Oliver don't forget me too quickly, will you? I wouldn't like that."

As if I ever could.

5 LUCY

*And the world's shrunken to a heap of hot flesh straining
on a bed.*

—E. R. Dodds

Khyber Street, when I returned, seemed more depressing than ever, squatting in the winter rain at the edge of the brickfield, black and ugly.

Slater was still not fit for duty, as Mr. Carter informed me on the first day of term, and I would be required to continue as before. Which didn't sit well with the top class at all, for they had been counting on Slater's return and a resumption of the old ways.

Things went from bad to worse during the first couple of weeks, and Varley and his friends were as difficult as it was possible to be. We were virtually back where we had started. To be honest, I had only myself to blame in some respects, for I had allowed the iron control I'd achieved during the previous term to slip more than a little.

I drifted in a mood of real depression, not caring very much about anything, I suppose, and missing Imogene. Strange how seldom we value what we have until we have lost it, and her replacement didn't help matters. She was a small, dark, eager girl of twenty-one who looked about sixteen and wore deceptively simple clothes that had obviously cost a great deal of money. She had one of those beautifully clipped upper-crust voices that only the better kind of English public school seems to be able to produce. In view of all this, it was hardly surprising that her name was Harriet. We spoke briefly at a general staff meeting. Carter had informed me that she lived in the Ladywood Park area, but when I raised the matter, she seemed dismayed more than anything else. My general impression being that she didn't care for me at all, I withdrew and left her severely alone.

But matters were fast approaching some sort of crisis with the top class. The flashpoint, when it came, was, as is usual in such affairs, the product of a rather trivial incident.

For the last day or two the weather had turned strangely warm for the time of year. It was muggy and oppressive, rain in the offing, but at least it was still dry, and I took the class out into the yard during a games period to play rounders.

Varley caused nothing but trouble from the start

for, as was to be expected, he was the sort of human being who was only interested in having the bat in his hand. Stage center or nothing.

He insisted on batting first for his team, worked his way around the bases and joined on at the end of the line of boys waiting to follow him. He kept glancing at me furtively, and I knew he intended to jump the queue as soon as he thought he could get away with it. I gave him a little rope, allowed him to bully his way three places up, but made no sign.

God, how I loathed him. And the things I had learned about him since our first meeting hardly improved matters. A vicious, mindless lout who had used that belt of his as a weapon on more than one occasion in gang fights, he had appeared in juvenile court twice and was at present on probation for breaking into the local youth club leader's flat, smashing everything in sight and defecating on the doormat as a grand finale. On top of everything else, he and his gang terrorized the entire district. *And Carter didn't want any trouble.*

Varley reached for the bat. I called, "Get back to the end of the queue and wait your turn, Varley."

"Who, me, sir?" There was outrage in his voice at the injustice of the suggestion.

"Yes, you," I told him firmly. "Get back to your proper place."

He threw the bat a good fifteen or twenty feet from him, turned and slouched toward the end of the queue.

"Wait for me in the corridor outside the class-room," I told him.

He glanced uncertainly from me to the class, realizing, I think, for the first time that when the chips were really down in any kind of public confrontation, he was on his own.

Perhaps I had pushed him too hard. One should always leave people a way out, some possibility of a retreat, but I was too young to be aware of that particular rule of life. He walked past me very slowly, insolence and defiance in every step. A yard or two away he started to whistle, then produced a comb and pulled it through his hair.

The class waited silently, not even a titter. There was an unnatural stillness. Somewhere thunder rumbled on the horizon, and the swollen gray belly of the clouds seemed ready to split wide open at any moment. I was hot, I was sweating and I'd very definitely had enough.

"Two seconds, Varley, to get through that door," I called. "That's all you've got."

The final end of things for him, too, I suppose, and he spun to face me, snarling. "Just you fucking well try to make me."

I started to run, he turned and made for the door too late. The flat of my hand caught him between the shoulder blades, sending him headfirst through the door to fall on his hands and knees by the steps.

I stood just inside the door, breathing hard. "Now get upstairs."

I was aware of the woodwork-room door opening, and Wally appeared. Varley crouched there for a moment, then came up suddenly, that belt of his free in his hand, the badges glinting. I managed to grab hold of the end before he could strike a blow, and threw it into the corner.

I can see his white, pinched face now as he

rushed at me in the gloom, the hatred blazing in his eyes for me, for the whole world. There was a flurry of ineffectual blows, one landing on my cheek rather unpleasantly; then he tried to put his knee into my groin. There seemed to be only one thing to do after that and I punched him in the stomach as hard as I could.

He doubled over in pain, and Wally grabbed him by the collar and ran him into the woodwork room, which was empty, for by chance Wally was enjoying a free period before taking my class next.

I stayed by the door, panting for breath, hands shaking. Wally shoved Varley down into a chair, came back and offered me a cigarette from an old battered silver case with some sort of regimental badge on the cover.

"What should I do?" I said as he gave me a light.

"No use going to Carter," he said. "You'll have to handle it yourself. Unless you want to make a police job of it." He picked up the belt. "They wouldn't have much difficulty in describing this as an offensive weapon."

"But you don't think I should?"

"Not unless you want them to do the job for you." He took out his pipe and filled it methodically. "I'll back you all the way, whatever you decide."

He had placed the belt over the end of the banister. I picked it up and nodded. "All right, give me five minutes with him. Then you can bring the rest of the class in."

He went out into the yard without further comment and I entered the woodwork room and closed the door.

Varley still sat in the chair into which Wally had

pushed him. I went behind the desk and stood looking down at him for a long moment. Then I threw the belt down with a crash.

"Assault with an offensive weapon. Borstal this time, Varley. A year, perhaps more. After all, you're on probation already. The bench won't like that."

"No, sir, please, sir! Don't get the police, sir! I didn't mean it!"

"Mr. Oldroyd should make an excellent witness," I went on relentlessly.

He broke then, came apart at the seams and started to sob, a harsh, ugly sound, tears oozing from his eyes. There are those who would say that he was not responsible for what he was. That I should have been sorry for him. Instead, I felt sickened by the very sight of him. He had given me hell for weeks and I was determined to have him off my back at all costs.

"All right," I said. "No police. You leave at Easter, don't you?"

"Yes, sir."

"Right, then you're on probation as far as I'm concerned. The slightest hint of trouble, and Mr. Oldroyd and I will take the whole story to the headmaster, which means no letter of recommendation when you leave. You try getting a job without one."

There was a knock at the door and Wally poked his head in. I nodded and he opened it further to allow the rest of the class to file past him solemnly. They stood behind their benches and waited expectantly.

"Varley has something to say," I told them. "Haven't you, Leonard?"

He ran his nose along his sleeve and stood up to face his final humiliation. "I'm sorry, sir," he said in a muffled tone, "for the way I behaved. It won't happen again, sir."

I walked out then, nodding briefly to Wally and left him to it. My legs felt weak as I climbed the stairs, no strength in them at all. The staff room was empty, which was a blessing, and I went into the lavatory and was promptly sick in the bowl.

My hands were still shaking and I felt degraded by the whole wretched business. I lit a cigarette and sat in a chair by the staff-room window. Thunder rumbled again and it started to rain. I looked out over the mean roofs below and at the squalor around me. It was enough. There had to be something better than this and I knew that I must get out at all costs.

• • •

In a sense, all I really did was follow Imogene's advice, and I returned to my writing with renewed vigor, into the small hours on occasion, sitting up there in the turret room at my table by the window, the whole world quiet outside.

I discovered I had a gift, if that is the correct term for it, for hard, sustained, creative work. Twenty thousand words in a week and all good stuff.

I decided to try something entirely different and as remote from Khyber Street and my general surroundings as possible. Looking for a subject, I returned to my old parody, however unintentional, of a Hemingway novel, and I discovered that whatever else it lacked of the great man's genius, it was in its essentials a good story.

I read each chapter through, then rewrote the whole, without any of its previous pretentiousness, as an honest and straightforward novel of adventure, reducing the original eighty thousand words to fifty. Finally I rounded it off with four new chapters.

Four weeks of incredibly hard work, mostly late at night, as I have said, but I still attended the Trocadero a couple of times a week, feeling the need · for relaxation and female companionship more than ever.

During this period I formed no new attachment, certainly nothing that lasted more than the particular evening involved. I saw several girls home after the dance, often traveling considerable distances by tram and frequently to no particular purpose. A kiss at the gate, or perhaps a little mild erotic byplay, to use one of Jake's favorite phrases, was my only reward, and usually I found myself faced with a long trudge back to Ladywood Park afterward, the last tram having gone.

I wondered seriously whether I was losing my touch but decided during some of those long walks home that the fault very probably lay in my own attitude. I hadn't really got over Imogene and, I suspect, did not have the heart for another such liaison as yet.

The only unusual incident during those weeks concerned a young, rather plain blond girl who claimed to be seventeen, but who, on reflection, was probably younger.

She lived in an area of rather pleasant old houses near the university, high walls and lots of trees. It was raining, as I recall and we had walked some considerable distance, discussing nothing more exciting than the latest films showing in the city.

I hadn't so much as put an arm around her waist, but when we stopped in a doorway and I kissed her, she started to tremble violently, then moaned a little and slid down the wall.

I grabbed her in alarm, thinking she was having an attack of some description, but to my amazement she opened her eyes, teeth chattering, and demanded to know, quite plainly, when I was going to do it to her. Such naivete had a certain charm, but it filled me with considerable alarm. I disentangled myself at the earliest possible moment and was away.

Jake, as usual, had some sort of explanation. "Nobody likes to have it offered on a plate, do they?" he said cheerfully. "I mean to say, where's the mystery? The adventure?"

"Maybe so," I said gloomily, "but the fact remains that I turned down a dead cert. What's wrong with me?"

"Maybe you liked Imogene more than you realized, old sport." He clapped me on the shoulder. "Never mind, spring will come again and you'll be standing up on end as well as you ever did."

• • •

I wrote the last chapter of the novel in a final burst of energy one Saturday afternoon, starting just after lunch, and finished at five minutes to seven. There still remained a certain amount of cleaning up to do and the final pages to type, but to all intents and purposes it was finished.

Tremendously elated, I hurried around to see Jake. As it happened he'd gone out for the evening, which in a sense left me with no one to tell, as Aunt Alice and Uncle Herbert were having tea with friends and she'd warned me not to expect them back till late.

Some sort of celebration was obviously in order so I got a couple of pounds from the tin box at the bottom of the wardrobe where I kept my mad money, walked to the park gates and caught a tram to The Tall Man.

By the time I arrived at the Trocadero, I was pretty tight, full of a fierce, nervous energy, which I suspect, was not simply the booze talking, but some sort of reactive process.

I hadn't been there on a Saturday for some time and had forgotten how crowded it could be. It was as rowdy as a fairground, with a hell of a lot of people on the floor for "Ballin' the Jack." I leaned against a pillar, smoking a cigarette, waiting for them to finish, and for a while the noise seemed to recede, leaving me washed up on some quiet shore on the periphery of things.

What on earth was I doing here? I asked myself. Who were these people? Faces. Looking back on all this, I believe that finishing the book had altered me in some fundamental way, an important step forward in the growth process, if you like, although I was not aware of it at the time and believed myself to be sinking into some quite unjustified depression.

I was pulled back to reality by an interesting little scene which was being enacted in front of me as the dance ended. A young woman was trying to pull away from a rather rough-looking specimen in a tight-waisted chalk-stripe suit who seemed to be insisting on hanging on to her hand. He had long black sideburns reaching to his jawline, in those days an infallible sign of the street-corner boy and the spiv.

A plain, round-faced girl with rather frizzy hair and horn-rimmed glasses, she had a nice voice, and was trying to be cheerful about it as she argued with him. As Jake used to say, all women are lovely in some way or other and Lucy had superb legs and a delightful bottom, nicely tight in a tweed skirt.

The trouble seemed to be that he was insisting she stay with him and wasn't taking no for an answer. Under normal circumstances I'd have minded my own business, but I'd had a drink or two, remember, and I'd seen Alan Ladd handle a similar situation with his usual competence in a film only the weekend before.

I moved in fast and took her free hand. "Oh, there you are. Sorry I've been so long."

She stayed surprisingly calm, her eyes behind the rather thick lenses of the glasses widening slightly, and then she smiled. "I'm dying for a coffee."

Sideburns glanced uncertainly at me. I gave him my best Alan Ladd deadpan look, cold, hard, a dangerous man to provoke, or so I hoped. It worked, or perhaps he just couldn't be bothered. In any event, he turned and faded into the crowd.

Whether he had believed in me as Alan Ladd was a moot point, but Lucy certainly did, for it became instantly plain that I had achieved a place of heroic stature in her eyes. From the expression on her face I thought she might ask me for my autograph at any moment.

"I just can't think what to say."

"Don't try," I said, at my most courtly, and led her on to the floor.

Where appearances are concerned, women are the most deceptive of all living things, and Lucy was an excellent example, for this plain, well-spoken, quiet young woman had a physical effect that left nothing to be desired. She had a sensuous body, that's what it mainly came down to, and she delighted in close contact, rubbing against me constantly, her cheek against mine.

It was completely unexpected, but that, if anything, only added to the excitement. I took her for coffee, we sat at a quiet corner table, and she leaned across to kiss me, one knee crossed over the other. I allowed my hand to rest on her thigh. She kissed me even more passionately, then excused herself, picked up her handbag and went to the cloakroom.

I lit another cigarette as I waited for her and sat there gazing down at the dancers, more than a little pleased at the way things had gone. This was exactly what I wanted. A warm, sensual woman who wanted me as much as I wanted her, needed a man, if you like, in a way that Imogene never had.

The truth is that by then, love, and I mean physical love and large amounts of it, had become the most exciting thing in the world for me, an experience which never palled and came up fresh as roses on a summer morning every time. Strangely enough, sitting there thinking about it, I was suddenly aware of some weird irrationally guilty feeling, which probably had its roots in long afternoons at Sunday school at the local Methodist chapel, lots of hellfire and damnation promised, and much reference, even at that tender age, to the consequences of indulging in the sins of the flesh. Lucy's reappearance soon swept that out of the way.

We had one more dance, a slow foxtrot which brought us even closer together. Although it was only ten o'clock, when I suggested that we leave early she agreed with alacrity and went off to get her coat.

· · ·

She lived in a cul-de-sac off the main road just past The Tall Man in a large semidetached house. There was a light on in the hall, but the glass sun porch was in darkness, and I slid my arms around her waist from behind, pulling her close. She gave a long, shuddering sigh, arching her back, then strained against me, turning up her face to be kissed. Her body trembled, emotion, I suppose, and she sighed again.

"You were so wonderful back there, Oliver. So incredible. I just couldn't believe it was happening."

"You don't think I could have stood by and left you to that oaf, do you? A girl like you?"

Which was perhaps a trifle melodramatic as remarks go, but it seemed to be the sort of thing she expected, and I slipped a hand inside her coat and started to stroke her left breast. And then the unexpected happened. She disengaged herself, fiddled around with her handbag, produced a key and unlocked the front door. I shriveled instantly, the disappointment biting deep, but in the same instant things assumed an even rosier hue for she turned in the doorway, light streaming out from the hall. "You'll come in for a while, won't you?"

"Will it be all right?"

She nodded. "There's only my father, and he goes to bed early."

More promising than ever. I followed her into the hall and she opened a door to the left and led the way into a pleasant lounge. It was comfortably furnished with a fitted carpet and a three-piece suite. She switched on an electric fire and drew the curtains. "Take off your coat and make yourself at home," she said. "I'll get you a drink. I think there's some whiskey in the cupboard. Would that be all right?"

I assured her it would be just fine, and she found a glass and a cut-glass decanter and poured a generous measure, two good doubles combined. She would have made it more if I hadn't stopped her.

She was damned naive and so keen to please me. "Have I done it wrong?" she asked, eyes swimming anxiously behind the thick lenses. "Is that all right?"

I reassured her with a light kiss on the cheek. She excused herself for a moment and left the room. I sat down in one of the easy chairs to drink my whiskey. It was really very comfortable, the cushions overripe and stuffed with feathers. I got up to test the couch, which looked as if it might prove a more than satisfactory battleground, and Lucy came back.

I turned to my chair and knocked over a small occasional table with rather a clatter. She moved in quickly to right it. "Don't worry, my father's almost stone deaf. He takes his hearing aid out when he goes to bed."

She had got rid of her coat and was certainly considerably more attractive than I'd realized. The whiskey talking, I suppose, but as she stood up from righting the table, I put an arm around her waist and pulled her close. In my imagination she seemed to rotate in my hands sensuously, closing her eyes, lips parting slightly, her breasts swelling beneath the thin blouse.

She was trembling as she stood there waiting, and I was filled with a sudden fierce pleasure that I could move her in a way I had always signally failed to move Imogene. It had a very satisfactory feeling of rightness to it. I was the master here. Male above female, as it was ordained to be.

Wishful thinking or, more likely, the whiskey increasing its grip. I sat on the couch and pulled her down beside me, then I kissed her, tenderly but with considerable finesse, ready for the slow, careful buildup.

To this day, I am not too certain what happened. It was as if Lucy seemed to lose her balance, sliding off the edge of the couch, pulling me down on top of her. I got the distinct impression that she was trying to beat me off although her mouth stayed fastened to mine, the tongue darting in and out like a mad thing. Her legs threshed about constantly, and at one point I thought she was trying to put a knee into my crotch.

Suddenly I realized that by some mysterious alchemy, she had managed to remove her pants. Her thighs spread on either side of me, knees raised. "It's all right," she murmured into my right ear in a surprisingly matter-of-fact tone. "I've put my diaphragm in."

Which fact alone should have occasioned me some suspicion, but by then I was thoroughly aroused. Within seconds she started to shake in a series of spectacular explosions that seemed to follow each other like a chain reaction. I finally managed to break free, which took some doing, for she was as strong as a horse, and I rolled on my back for a moment, taking some very deep breaths.

She kissed my ear. "Gorgeous!" she whispered. "Absolutely heavenly."

She reached for me again and before I knew where I was, I was back on the job, working away manfully while Lucy continued to explode. I'd heard of such cases, had never experienced one until now.

When I broke free, she was still in full flight, but I had very definitely given my all. Like the man in the song, I was tired and I wanted to go home. But she wouldn't leave me alone.

What with that enormous whiskey on top of everything else I'd drunk that night, I just wasn't in any fit state to rise to the sort of occasion she seemed to demand. It didn't matter a bit, for the next thing I knew she was on top of me, legs straddled, skirt rising.

She trembled and shook, eyes closed, her face wreathed in ecstasy. I suddenly knew beyond any shadow of a doubt that I had stumbled across that creature who, in spite of the frequency with which she invades the sexual fantasies of the average male, is in reality a rare bird indeed. The insatiable woman who can't get enough of it.

She leaned down covering my face with moist, openmouthed kisses, and a door opened and closed again upstairs. She gave an extra shudder, then disengaged herself, stood up and pulled down her skirt.

She put a finger to her lips, moved to the door and opened it slightly. I buttoned myself up hurriedly and heard a toilet flush. A stair creaked as someone started to come down and she turned, face expressionless, and threw my trench coat to me. As I pulled it on, she picked up her pants, which were lying on the floor, and stuffed them under a cushion.

The door opened a moment later and a tall, skinny old man with the face of a desiccated monkey and yellow, watery eyes entered. He wore an old-fashioned quilted dressing gown of some sort of wine-colored silk, and there was a hearing aid in his right ear.

"Hello, darling, I thought you'd be asleep." Lucy kissed him on the cheek. "This gentleman was kind enough to escort me home."

He glared at me like some virulent adder, moved to the fireplace and tapped a finger on the clock.

"Gentleman?" he said in a dry old voice that suited his appearance admirably. "And what kind of gentleman, pray, keeps a young lady out after eleven o'clock at night?"

The end part of his little speech rose to a crescendo. It was all of ten past eleven. I was tired, and one thing was certain. After Lucy, I had nothing left over for scenes of this sort.

"I think I'd better be going," I said and edged toward the door. Lucy spoke to him briefly in a low voice. It sounded as though she said, "I think you should apologize, George," but that didn't seem likely.

"Oh, very well," he muttered and raised his voice

to call as I reached the door, "Perhaps I was a little hasty. Thank you for seeing my wife home safely. It was most kind of you."

"My pleasure." I said and got out fast.

Lucy had me by the sleeve as I went through the porch. "Please, Oliver, give me a minute."

She closed the door. We were alone in the warm darkness. "You are one for the book, aren't you?" I said.

"Lucille?" he shouted querulously from inside.

"The master calls," I said unkindly and opened the outside porch door.

She held on tight. "Can I meet you somewhere tomorrow?"

"Good God!" I said, "You really take the biscuit, don't you?"

"Please, Oliver, it's a lot more complicated than it looks."

She moved close, very close, the tops of those good breasts nudging my chest, and then she put a hand on my arm again. It was all she had to offer, poor girl, I could see that. On the other hand, I wanted to get away, and there was only one means of accomplishing that.

"All right," I said. "Where and when?"

"Ladywood Park gates. One-thirty tomorrow afternoon. Is that all right?"

When I nodded, she kissed me passionately again, and then the old man started creating a fuss inside and she opened the door and went in.

• • •

"Nymphomaniac?" Jake said. "Don't make me laugh. It's all sailors' tales like mermaids and the unicorn."

126

"And a sea of pitch on the other side of the Cape of Good Hope?" I said.

"Exactly."

He turned from making the tea and yawned as he walked to the window. He looked tired, too tired really, but it was understandable. His final exams were in three or four weeks. It was make-or-break time.

"You don't think it exists, then?" I persisted. "As a condition, I mean?"

"Oh, there's a hell of a difference in frequency pattern, I'll grant you that." He poured the tea and spooned in condensed milk. "Sex is an appetite just like food and drink, and some people like to indulge more than others."

"Then what's the norm?" I demanded.

"There's no such animal. Anything from once a year to three times a day if you can find someone to put up with you."

He sat in the window seat and filled his pipe. I said, "And what about Lucy?"

"God knows." He shrugged. "Young girl married to an old man. That's an old story. She was probably making up months of frustration in one grand slam tonight."

Which was always possible. I sat there thinking about it. He said, "What about tomorrow? Are you going to go?"

"I hadn't intended to. What do you think?"

"Oh, give her a chance," he said. "Everyone deserves that. On the other hand, I'm too tired to think straight, so don't blame me if it goes sour on you."

It started to rain again as I crossed the garden on

my way home, but then it had been that kind of winter. No snow at all.

When I went into the bedroom, everything was exactly as I had left it—the typescript of my book stacked neatly beside the portable typewriter, the final sheet still in the machine. For the first time in weeks there was nothing to do, no personal demon to drive me on. I went to bed and slept, in spite of the night's exertions, extremely badly.

* * *

I spent the morning working hard on the editing of the book, had an early lunch, and was at the park gates in good time for our rendezvous. I worked my way through the *Sunday Dispatch* as I waited.

There was nothing of any great moment in the news. Milk rationing was to be suspended, hotels and restaurants freed of the five-shilling meal rule. They'd certainly taken their time over that considering the war had been over nearly five years. Not surprisingly, there was to be a general election. I stuffed the newspaper into a wastepaper basket and stepped back hastily as a prewar Austin Seven pulled in at the curb, Lucy at the wheel.

"Sorry I'm late," she called and opened the door for me. "Hop in."

I squeezed into the passenger seat. "This yours?"

She shook her head. "No, my husband's. It stood in the garage on wood blocks most of the war."

She had made her face up very carefully and wore a blue reefer jacket with naval buttons, a Black Watch tartan skirt, tan stockings and brown brogues. She really did look very nice.

Lucy

"I thought we might go for a drink," she said. "If that's all right?"

Which was fine by me. I sat back and left it to her and she took me to a little country pub about five minutes' drive away in a village just outside the city boundary, the sort of place that was certain to be swallowed up by Greater Manningham once private building really got going again.

We had the snug to ourselves. I got her the gin and tonic she asked for and a pint of bitter for myself and we sat in an old-fashioned wooden booth by the window, knees touching.

"This is nice," she said, looking around the room.

"Haven't you been here before?"

"Oh, yes," she nodded. "I came here several times with my mother, but that was a long time ago. Nineteen forty-five."

"The year the war ended."

"That's right. She was killed in a car crash three weeks after V.E. day with an Australian squadron leader she'd been running around with."

She didn't seem particularly upset, so I said carefully, "What about your father?"

"Oh, he died years ago. Before the war. Some kind of cancer, I think. Here, let me get you another drink." She took my glass before I could protest and was away. She came back with another gin and tonic for herself and a whiskey and soda for me, a double from the taste of it. "I thought you might fancy a change."

I made no comment. Instead, I said, "What about your husband? When did you meet him?"

"He lived next door to us for years. I was seven-

129

teen when my mother died, and she left me nothing but debts. I was working in an insurance office as a junior clerk. Two pounds five shillings a week. Anything would have been better."

She traced a finger along the top of my thigh to my kneecap idly, still staring out of the window. I said, "Why did he marry you?"

"God knows. Not to sleep with me if that's what you're thinking. He was sixty-seven when we married, and a bad heart to boot. A whim of the moment maybe. Who knows?"

But there were other, possibly darker reasons, I was certain of that, and was just as certain that she had told me all she intended. Not that it mattered. One pint of best bitter plus a double whiskey and I fancied her again.

I put a hand on her knee. "No more sad songs. It's a lovely afternoon. Let's go for a walk."

"I know just the place," she said and kissed me full on the mouth.

• • •

We drove out in the general direction of Haxby, keeping to the back roads and moving through some glorious countryside. As I've already said, it had been a curiously mild winter and here we were on a Sunday in February that had all the ingredients of an October autumnal. Blackbirds picking over the bones of plowed fields. A haze over things, a gentleness, a touch of woodsmoke in the air.

She turned the car into a narrow, rutted track which ran between high hedges and stopped beside a five-barred gate after a couple of hundred yards.

"There's a wood on the other side," she said

when we got out. "Very pleasant. No one ever comes up here. There's a rug on the back seat, by the way."

She seemed to have everything nicely organized. I helped her over the stile beside the gate, and we moved along the lane. There was another stile at the boundary fence of the wood, and as we negotiated it, rooks lifted like black rags out of the beech trees overhead, calling angrily.

She left the path after a while and struck off through the trees as if she knew exactly what she was doing. She did, actually, because within two or three minutes we came to a sun-dappled clearing between rocks that might have been made for the job.

"This is nice," I said.

"Yes, isn't it?"

I wondered how many others she'd been here with as I spread the rug neatly. Not that it seemed to matter. I took her in my arms and kissed her, and within seconds we were at it again, a repeat performance of the previous night.

Her tartan skirt was a wraparound, which was certainly convenient, and her blouse worked on the same principle, being tied at the waist. When I unfastened it, it opened to disclose the rather pleasant fact that she wasn't wearing a bra. I kissed her breasts, she grabbed my head, crushing my face against her, and spread her legs. There was the same monotonous series of trembling explosions, the same gasps and moans.

I recall reading once of some medieval priest being tried for witchcraft who complained piteously that each night an insatiable succubus came to him in his cell and forced him to perform the physical act repeatedly. I know how he must have felt, for Lucy simply couldn't be satisfied. She rattled away relentlessly, seemingly endowed with an inexhaustible supply of energy.

I surfaced to stare up at sunlight dappling the trees, a considerable part of me one big ache. I became aware, after a while, that she was starting again, and some instinct for survival surfaced to give me the strength to push her away and force myself to my knees.

"Sorry," I mumbled. "Taken short. Only be a moment."

She stretched languorously, one knee raised, the skirt around her waist, and the afternoon sun touched her breasts with fire. I moved into the trees. God knows what was needed to satisfy Lucy, but I certainly wasn't up to the job. I imagined her lying on the rug back there in the clearing waiting for more.

"Hurry up, darling," she called.

It was enough. I dropped to my hands and knees and crept from tree to tree like an Indian. When I was far enough away, I simply took to my heels and ran for my life.

•   •   •

Jake was sitting by the fire working his way through the Sunday papers when I opened the door and staggered in.

"Good God!" he said. "What have you been up to?"

"Remember that thing you said didn't exist?" I said.

Lucy

"The unicorn?"

I nodded and sank into the chair opposite him. "Well, it does, Jake. Oh, God, but it bloody well does."

6 OLIVE

All wickedness is but little to the wickedness of a woman.
—Apocrypha, Ecclesiasticus

Uncle Herbert died quite peacefully in his sleep one night toward the end of February, his tired old heart finally giving up the struggle.

He must have been marked down as long overdue wherever it is you report in, and yet it was difficult in some ways to believe him gone, especially when I went into the bedroom with Aunt Alice to see him laid out in his best blue serge suit, white linen shirt and regimental tie. He looked extremely

135

peaceful, a little shrunken perhaps, but otherwise much as usual.

"You'd think he was only sleeping," I whispered.

"Of course he is," Aunt Alice said calmly. "Death doesn't exist. Not for those who truly care for each other and have faith."

There wasn't much I could say to that so I simply squeezed her hand and led her outside. She brushed my hair back from my eyes with one hand.

"You're a good boy, Oliver. He was very proud of you, particularly that degree of yours, and he wouldn't want you to grieve without reason, so don't." She kissed me on the cheek. "I'll arrange a seance soon. There are certain to be messages. Herbert and I always promised that whoever passed first would communicate with the other."

None of this sounded particularly dotty, for I'd been raised on it, although that doesn't mean I believed it more than I believed in any of the standard religious explanations of the universe and the state of man.

We gave him a nice funeral with a burial service at the local Methodist church, and they found him a plot in the corner of the graveyard by the wall under an elm tree close to the old First World War monument with the incredibly long list of names. *The Unconquered,* that's what it said on the bronze plaque at the base. *They battled, they endured, they died.* He must have been lonely for a long, long time.

There weren't many of us there. Aunt Alice and me, Jake and his mother, half a dozen old family friends, and halfway through the service Herr Nagel turned up.

It rained quite hard and I held an umbrella over Aunt Alice as we each tossed a handful of soil, and the clergyman droned bravely on in the certain hope of the resurrection and the life.

But I was not so confident. Not then or later, when I slipped away from the ham-and-salad tea at the house and went down to the conservatory he had loved so much to say a sort of private goodbye. His orchids were still there. They endured, which was some slight comfort, I suppose.

• • •

Just over a week before Uncle Herbert's death I received a letter from my literary agent. The book was fine. Quite definitely publishable, although he suggested a minor but significant alteration in the ending—a question of whether the heroine survived or not.

I was so excited that I sat up all night, rewrote the final chapter, then typed out a fair copy including two carbons, as with the original. I walked out into the cool dawn feeling tremendously elated and had the whole thing on its way back to him by the seven-thirty post.

The day after the funeral, he wrote again to say that the chapter was all that he had hoped. He now had the book out to a well-known publishing firm and had sent one of the carbon copies to their New York office in hope of an American sale. The other was now being read by the agent's colleague who specialized in film rights.

I went around to see Jake instantly, brandishing the letter, but found him curiously reticent. It occurred to me then that he might in some way resent this hint of good fortune, considering his own lack of success in the literary field so far, but I dismissed the idea as being unworthy.

In fact, I was closer to the truth than I had realized, for many years later he confessed as much to me at a memorable reunion. By then, of course, we could laugh about it, as he had become one of the most successful television playwrights in the country.

●　●　●

Aunt Alice arranged the seance she had mentioned for one Saturday evening. I managed to obtain an invitation for Jake, who was much more available now, having taken his final examinations, although it would be some weeks before he'd know the results.

She had imported the medium from London especially for the occasion, an imposing gentleman in a beautifully tailored dark-gray flannel suit that looked suspiciously Savile Row to me, which indicated he was hardly having to scrape for a living. He had a thin, intelligent face the color of dark walnut and luminous eyes. An unusual feature was his black turban. I never did catch his name, for everyone referred to him quite simply, and with considerable reverence, as "Swami."

Tea and cakes were served in the dining room beforehand, and Aunt Alice looked as spectacular as usual in that housecoat of hers embroidered with the signs of the zodiac, her jet-black hair hanging straight to her shoulders.

The only other male present was Herr Nagel, who was possibly back in favor again. I hoped so, for on the occasions I had spoken to him, I had found beneath the rather comic Prussian mannerisms a benign, kindly man who took his astrology very seriously and was engaged in a scientific study of the whole business. In fact, he had nearly converted me.

The rest of the party consisted of half a dozen ladies, all friends of Aunt Alice's. There was one who interested me particularly, addressed by the others as Olive. She must have been well into her forties, as that seemed the general age range, yet she exuded a powerful sexuality that was accentuated by a dress in a black crepey material that clung to her curves.

In fact, everything about her was the same color from the hair hanging straight to the shoulders to the stockings and high-heeled patent-leather shoes.

"My God!" Jake whispered. "She'd swallow you whole, that one."

"Do you think so?" I said, for, to be honest, I found her faintly disturbing.

He nodded. "Reminds me of one of those spiders that eats its young."

We were playing polite young men, moving among the ladies with plates of cakes. I went to the kitchen on one occasion to replenish the stock, for the good ladies had healthy appetites in spite of their obsession with the other world. I found Aunt Alice making a fresh pot of tea and asked her about Olive.

She was a very dear friend, it seemed, a widow lady who admitted to forty-two. Her husband had left her a small engineering firm in the city so she was well provided for. She lived near the golf course.

I was regaling Jake with these facts on my return when I suddenly realized that the lady in question was watching us speculatively. When she caught my eye she bore down on us at once.

"And what brings you two boys here?" she demanded. "I didn't think the young had time for such serious interests."

I explained who I was and introduced Jake. Not that it mattered, for she seemed to be one of those people who forget names in an instant, and she became hopelessly confused during the conversation which followed, on several occasions addressing Jake as if it were he who was Aunt Alice's nephew, not me.

There was one touch of color about her—the wide, petulant mouth which had been accentuated in vivid scarlet. Even the pendant that hung around her neck was jet, and it nestled at the end of its chain in the valley between breasts that were rather alarmingly revealed by her plunging neckline.

"What *should* we be interested in then?" Jake inquired at one point.

"Oh, come now," she said. "What are young men always interested in? The opposite sex."

"Don't you approve?" I asked her.

"In a meeting of equals," she said. "Nothing less. You men have been treading us into the dirt for years, forcing us to meet your needs, not ours, isn't that so?"

She seemed to be gazing at me with a peculiar intensity. Jake choked, excused himself and fled. She turned as if to move away herself and stumbled. I steadied her instantly and she put a hand on my arm.

"How strong you are. So few young men take care

140

of their bodies. It's a sin against nature. You look after yourself?"

"I like to keep fit," I said wildly. "I go for a run in the park before breakfast every morning." Which was true, as it happened. "Twice around the lake."

"When were you born?"

"July."

"I'm so glad." Her eyes widened. "I am a Scorpio, did you know that? Sign of regeneration."

God knows what was coming next, but I was saved by Aunt Alice's clapping her hands briskly and calling us into the drawing room.

• • •

The velvet drapes were drawn, cutting out any possibility of light from outside, although it was almost dark by that time. There was a large circular table in the center of the room, a Victorian piece in mahogany, especially purchased by Aunt Alice for such occasions. Ten chairs were arranged around it.

All of this was perfectly familiar to me as I had helped her set the scene for the affair earlier in the day. The one extra was a trumpet-shaped object painted dull silver, which was very carefully positioned in the center of the table on a square of black velvet.

Jake and I lurked around at the rear waiting to see what would happen. Aunt Alice started things off by welcoming everyone.

"And I would just like to say on behalf of all here," she added, turning to the chief guest, "how lucky we are to have the Swami tonight all the way from London. I'm sure he will reveal many wonderful things to us."

The ladies murmured their appreciation and the Swami placed the palms of his hands together and made a formal gesture of obeisance.

"And now I believe the Swami would like to say a few words before we begin."

The gentleman in question spoke quite excellent English, but with almost a Welsh intonation, as I have frequently noted with Indians. He seemed to be under some kind of stress, his fingers tightly interlaced as he glanced from one face to another.

"I must ask," he said suddenly, grinding his teeth together, "all unbelievers to leave the room."

There followed what may only be described as a pregnant pause during which most of the ladies stirred uneasily. I glanced at Jake, who stood, hands folded, poker-faced. Herr Nagel nodded benignly as if to reassure me.

"Yes, leave the room!" The Swami's voice cracked and he flung out one arm, finger pointing at the door. "For my life, my very existence, will be in the gravest danger if a single mocker remains."

Which as far as I was concerned screwed the coffin lid down tight, but I wouldn't have missed the rest of the proceedings for anything. He closed his eyes tightly, hands together, muttered what I could only conclude to be a prayer and motioned us to the table, where I found myself on Olive's right. Jake was on her other side.

A few of the ladies held hands and the Swami shook his head. "No, palms flat on the table in front of you, please. If there is any contact tonight, the spirits will speak to us through the trumpet. Perhaps in one corner of the room, perhaps another."

"You mean the trumpet's going to float through the air?" asked Jake in some amazement.

"But of course," the Swami said calmly. "Do not be alarmed. There is nothing to fear. But no one must move while I am in trance, I cannot stress that too much. Any untoward movement could have tragic effects for me."

Which seemed a trifle illogical if one considered how much happier things were on the other side, according to him and his friends. Herr Nagel got up and stood by the light switch at the door, that benign smile still on his face. The Swami nodded, the light went out. There was a slight pause for Herr Nagel to reach his seat, and then the proceedings got under way.

The trumpet had obviously been painted with some sort of luminous paint and it glowed faintly, so that the surrounding darkness seemed blacker than ever. I really couldn't see a thing. I sat there waiting, palms flat against the table, listening to the Swami's stertorous breathing.

It finally faded away in a dying fall, leaving only the silence. A moment or so later, the trumpet rose slowly into the air.

• • •

At the same time, a hand was placed upon my left knee, which anchored me to earth, so to speak, considerably reducing the shock I might normally have been expected to feel at the more mystical turn events had taken.

Not that there was anything of the spirit about that hand which crawled purposefully up my thigh. It could only be Olive, and I sat there, petrified, in the darkness, palms flat on the table, eyes glued to the trumpet, which was now moving away toward the other end of the parlor about six or seven feet above the floor.

Invisible fingers were busying themselves, found what they were searching for a moment later, and then fate intervened as dramatically as possible. There was one hell of a clatter out there in the darkness, the trumpet waved wildly, then nose-dived into the ground.

"Jesus Christ Almighty!" someone cried in ripest cockney.

The hand was withdrawn at once. I pushed my chair back, and as I stood, the lights were turned on by Herr Nagel, who was at the door.

The Swami was sprawled across a fallen chair, a chair which I had last seen standing beside the door when Herr Nagel had switched off the lights. I could only conclude that my Teutonic friend was faster on his feet than he looked.

"Who put the bleeding chair 'ere?" the Swami demanded, trying to sit up.

Jake and I went to his assistance and put him on his feet again. As I brushed him down, he tried to retrieve the situation.

"An unfortunate occurrence, my friends," he began, back in character again.

But he was wasting his time, he knew that, and he faltered into silence under the collective stare of the ladies, who gazed at him in dismay, disgust or anger, according to temperament and inclination.

"How could I have been so deceived?" Aunt Alice demanded bitterly, an awe-inspiring sight with the rage on her, Hecuba, Joel and the great goddess Kali rolled into one.

"Dear lady." Herr Nagel moved in front of her rapidly. "Calm yourself, I beg of you."

He kissed her hand passionately, then turned and advanced on the Swami who immediately backed toward the door in alarm, reverting to his true self on the instant.

"All right, I'm going," he said hastily. "No need for the heavy brigade."

There was some sort of scuffle out in the hall, then the front door banged. Herr Nagel appeared a moment later. Aunt Alice tucked a hand in his arm and turned to address the rest of the party.

"If you'll all come into the dining room, I think a little sherry might be in order. I can't tell you how sorry I am at the way things turned out."

She went through the door on Herr Nagel's arm and the others followed. I had been watching Olive closely but she made not the slightest sign, staring past me in a bored sort of way, and I began to wonder whether the whole thing might not have been an hallucination. Jake picked up the trumpet, which the Swami had forgotten, due to the hurried nature of his departure, and put it on the table. He seemed strangely preoccupied.

"Souvenir of an interesting evening," I said and added, "You've got a couple of fly buttons undone."

"So have you, if it comes to that," he told me.

In the act of adjusting ourselves we paused and stared at each other. "My God!" Jake said. "You, too?"

Through the open door Olive's voice rose above the noise in the next room as they started to pass the sherry. "But surely it is the spiritual in all things that must be searched for in every area of existence," she said clearly. "I mean, we're all agreed on that, aren't we?"

"A drink," Jake whispered. "A very large one. That's what I need."

We crept into the hall, let ourselves out the front door and left them to it.

• • •

The morning run in the park was a habit I had only developed during the weeks since finishing the novel, as a release, a way of using up surplus energy. It was certainly not part of any deliberate physical fitness program.

The truth is, I liked the early-morning smell of things, mist on the lake, a drift of rain through the trees, the feeling that somehow I had the whole day to myself. The morning after the seance I awoke just before seven with a bad taste in my mouth and a slight headache, thanks to an extended pub crawl with Jake the night before.

Rain drummed against the turret windows relentlessly. It was Sunday. I could stay in bed as long as I wanted. Perhaps for that very reason, perhaps because I had a choice, I got up, pulled on my old tracksuit and a pair of basketball boots, crept downstairs and let myself out the back door.

The rain was really quite torrential—not that I minded as I cut down the hill from the playing fields and followed the path around the lake to the woods on the far side.

The rain brought out the best in me, as it always did, and I jogged along cheerfully, thinking about the book and wondering how things were going. It had already been rejected by two publishers although the agent had assured me that this was part of the general pattern of things and only to be expected. He had followed this by quoting, to comfort me, the names of several best-sellers all rejected by someone or other in their time. All right, two I could accept, but three . . .

The rain so obscured my glasses that it wasn't worth wearing them and I slipped them into my pocket. The result was that the figure ahead of me as I rounded the far end of the lake was just a blur that didn't turn into a woman until I was ten or fifteen yards away. I was virtually on top of her before I realized it was Olive.

She wore Wellington boots, a black oilskin raincoat with matching sou'wester, and carried, rather incongruously, a large, multicolored golfing umbrella. A small black poodle trailed after her at the end of a chain lead looking thoroughly miserable.

"Hello there," I said brightly.

She stared at me, frowning slightly. "Alice Shaw's nephew," I said helpfully. "Oliver. The seance last night. Surely you remember?"

She seemed vaguely surprised. "I thought you had fair hair?"

"That was my friend."

She made no further comment but started to walk again, following the lakeside path to where it branched to climb the hill. I walked beside her, wondering whether I ought to clear off, for I was uncertain of my ground here although it seemed more than a coincidence that she should appear like this so soon after our last meeting.

She paused in the shelter of a large beech tree and closed the umbrella. "Do you do this often?" she said calmly. "This running?"

I was conscious of a momentary irritation at this new ploy and wondered what on earth she was playing at. It was so childish to pretend she didn't know. Still, if she wanted to play the game this way . . .

"Most mornings," I said patiently. "It's good for me."

She made no answer, but produced a silver case and lighter from one of her pockets and offered me a cigarette. We smoked in silence for a few moments. The rain thundered into the lake, a continuous rushing sound that filled the morning.

I was close to making my excuses and clearing off, having had enough of the whole weird business, but turning, I found her watching me, a strange, intent look on her face.

"You really are wet, aren't you?" She bunched the front of my tracksuit in one hand, squeezed and water ran out. "Have you much further to go?"

"Another couple of miles should do it," I said. "Across the golf course and back home along Shire End."

"I live at number three," she said. "The detached house with the bench and white gables."

Until that moment I felt nicely in command and, to be frank, was more interested in the mechanics of the thing than the eventual outcome. She fingered my tracksuit again. "Yes, absolutely soaking. What you need is a nice hot drink."

She gazed past me into space, a slight, abstracted frown on her face, her fingers still experimenting with the moisture content of the tracksuit, working their way steadily downward. For a moment, time stood still and I was sixteen again, alternating between the twin delights of tobacco and sexual pleasure at Wilma's gentle hands.

Olive brought me back to the present by suddenly kissing me. And what a kiss. The mouth opened wide, her hand hooked painfully into the hair at the back of my head. "The best tunes are played on the oldest fiddles"—I'd read that somewhere. And then she pulled away from me and put her umbrella up briskly.

"I'll have it waiting for you," she said. "Don't forget."

By which she meant, I presumed, the hot drink. I watched her go, the multicolored umbrella bobbing through the trees, and remembered what Jake had predicted. That she looked like the kind of woman who would want to swallow you whole.

On the other hand, it was certainly a much more stimulating way of spending Sunday morning than lying in bed working one's way through the newspapers. I took to my heels and ran up through the wood toward the golf course in a mood of what I can only describe as cheerful anticipation.

• • •

It was just nearing eight o'clock when I reached the house in Shire End, crack o'dawn for Ladywood Park on a Sunday morning. I didn't see a soul, not even a paperboy—although they usually delivered a lot later than that on weekends.

I went in through the back gate to keep things reasonably private and approached the rear of the house, which was an excellent specimen of what in

Yorkshire we call "woolbrokers' Tudor," the gables painted, as she had indicated, in black and white. I went through a little patio and rang the bell at the kitchen door.

After a while a window opened above my head and Olive peered out. I stepped back from the door to reveal myself. "Oh, it's you." she said. "Go around to the front and let yourself in. And don't forget to take those filthy boots off."

I removed my basketball boots on the porch and went into the house barefoot, the ironbound oak door opening at a touch. I found myself in a large, gloomy hall with a polished woodblock floor, a staircase to the left, a stained-glass window to one side against which the rain tapped ceaselessly for admission.

I stood there, water dripping into a pool around my feet, and Olive said, "My goodness, you are wet, aren't you?"

She was standing on the landing at the turn of the stairs looking down at me, dressed exactly as she had been the previous night in the crepe dress with the plunging neckline, black stockings and patent-leather shoes. It was a hair-raising sight for that time of day, and I couldn't think of a thing to say. I simply stood there staring up at her.

"Come on up!" she said. "I'll get you a towel."

I followed with alacrity, but she had disappeared when I reached the top landing. I hesitated, called her name and moved forward, and at the same moment realized that the door on my left stood open.

It was a beautiful bedroom. Wall-to-wall carpet in palest green to match the walls, mahogany furniture, rich-looking, well polished, and the largest bed I'd ever seen in my life, with a couple of white Turkish towels draped over the end.

Olive stood in front of the wardrobe mirror, tightening a garter, her dress pulled up.

The scene was consciously posed, of course, and entirely for my benefit, reminiscent of the photos to be found in a certain kind of pinup magazine, although I had no intention of holding that against her. She glanced up and watched me for a moment, the skirt still bunched, that strangely intent look on her face again as if curious to see what my reaction would be.

"Oh, there you are," she said after a moment and smoothed down her dress. "I've got some towels here. You'd better get that wet tracksuit off."

To be honest, I was interested to see how this curious game of hers was to develop, and only she knew that. So, for the present, I did as I was told, unzipped the top half of my tracksuit and pulled it off.

As I picked up one of the towels and started to dry my hair, she said with a slight touch of exasperation, "You silly boy, what good's half a loaf?"

My head was buried in the towel at the time, and before I could disentangle it she had hauled my pants down. There was a kind of gasp, and when I got rid of the towel, I found her sitting on the edge of the bed staring mesmerized at what she had revealed. I was not surprised; in spite of the fact that I was wearing a jockstrap, it hardly proved equal to the occasion for, to use another grand old Yorkshire saying, I was standing up like a chapel-hat peg.

"Oh, my God, how awful," she said and reached out, her hand shaking slightly.

By this time I'd had enough of the preliminaries and grabbed for her, but she pulled away so that I lost my balance and fell on one knee. To my amazement, she crossed her knees, pulling her skirt up high, and presented one shining patent-leather shoe.

"Kiss it!" she commanded imperiously.

The idea didn't appeal to me in the slightest, a healthy sign, I hope, and I told her so.

"Do as I say," she said angrily, "or I'll never buy my newspapers from you again."

Which pretty definitely confirmed my suspicions that our Olive was a very peculiar lady indeed.

"I'm afraid you've got the wrong boy," I said. "Maybe he comes Saturdays."

She sprawled back on the bed, a hand to her forehead. "You're all the same. Brutes, all of you. I suppose you'll be wanting to tie me up next and beat me."

"With meat rationing the way it is? You've got to be kidding," I said, gay and jocular to the end, and reached for my tracksuit.

She had an arm around my neck before I knew what was happening, her mouth fastening on mine greedily, and she pulled me back across the bed on top of her. For a moment I thought it was going to be all right after all, and then she groaned and writhed like a mad thing for a few seconds, and that was very much that.

I started to get up and she held me close, her eyes wide. "You can have one now," she said.

But by then all I wanted to do was get out. "No, thanks," I said. "I must be off. My breakfast will be getting cold."

She lay on the bed glaring at me as I pulled on my tracksuit, and I left her without a second glance and padded downstairs.

As I crossed the hall, she called from the landing "All the same, beasts, all of you. Don't you ever come here again."

That I could have promised her, hand on heart.

I pulled on my basketball boots and went down the drive. As I reached the front gate, the newspaper boy appeared, a tall, gangling, pimply youth of seventeen or so wearing a parka. I glanced back and saw Olive standing in the porch watching, and I waved cheerfully.

"I'd hurry up if I were you," I told the astonished lad. "She can't wait to get her hands on your papers this morning."

His jaw dropped, as they say, but I was already running away into the rain before he could reply.

7 HARRIET

Girls like to be played with and rumpled a little, too, sometimes.

—Oliver Goldsmith

For a while things seemed to be pretty much at a standstill, and this was certainly true as far as the book front was concerned. I moved, or drifted, through life like a sleepwalker, and nothing had any reality at all. Jake had been transferred by his firm to its London office, which left an enormous gap. I felt more than usually at a loss, waiting, I suppose, for it all to happen, or not to happen.

I had done everything that I could in any personal sense. The rest was now up to fate, time and chance, the lesser gods, or whatever other intangibles rule over the lives of men.

As for Khyber Street, I simply soldiered on, one day very much like another. I was used to the place by now, of course, and it was used to me, but that happens in life and is to be expected.

Slater of the broken leg had finally returned, complete with walking stick, to limp around the place a little more heavily than I thought was necessary. He assured us all at frequent intervals that the doctor had not wanted him to return, but he, Slater, had insisted, knowing full well what a burden his absence was proving to the rest of the staff.

I suspect that he had some sneaking hope that Carter, out of regard for his condition, might give him an easier class, and I was resigned to being told to carry on with the top class myself, especially as it was only two weeks to Easter.

Carter, with his usual perversity, did exactly the opposite of what was expected. Slater, to the great joy of Varley and company, was back behind his old desk on the following Monday morning, and I found myself acting as relief teacher, giving some free time each day to all other members of staff in turn.

• • •

The boys in the top class reverted to their old ways with a vengeance for the brief period of school life remaining to them. Carter was obviously not prepared to do anything about it, indeed pretended that the situation didn't exist.

I felt sorry for Slater, who was unable to exercise any kind of control, but there was little that anyone could do. I took them each day for a couple of periods, and they were as good as gold. The moment Slater limped back in, all hell broke loose.

Things really came to a head on the final day of term, which, for obvious reasons, no one was particularly looking forward to. The staff room was full of sinister tales of the excesses committed by past leavers on their final day.

I took most of these tales with a pinch of salt until about twelve-thirty, the middle of the lunch break. I was sitting in the staff room having a cup of tea and a sandwich with Schwartz and Johnson when there was a resounding crash from another part of the building, followed by another crash. From the look on Schwartz's face, he expected the Gestapo to break through the door at any moment, and Johnson turned pale.

"My God!" he said. "They've started."

The door opened and Slater, who had been on corridor duty, lurched in and collapsed into the nearest chair wiping sweat from his face.

"They've ripped several lights out of the ceiling in my classroom," he said, his voice uneven.

"Did you see who it was?" I demanded.

He shook his head. "Gone by the time I got there."

I went downstairs to take a look. The place really was a shambles, with broken glass everywhere, and the contents of Slater's desk had been tipped out and literally douched with urine.

Slater limped in through the open door behind me followed by Wally Oldroyd and Carter, who had just returned from a meeting at the Education Offices. Wally looked around the room, his face grim, but Carter simply nodded, coughing over his cigarette as usual.

"I really do think you should be able to exercise more control over them than this, Mr. Slater."

I controlled my anger at that one with difficulty and contented myself by saying, "As good a case as we'll ever have for calling in the police."

For a moment, I thought he might faint. He turned very white and put a hand to the door to steady himself.

"The police?" he said. "In my school? Don't be absurd. They're leaving, aren't they? They're walking out through that gate at four o'clock this afternoon never to return."

There was a slight pause during which Wally filled and lit his pipe methodically, giving nothing away. Carter glanced from one face to the other seeking comfort and support.

"I mean, you do see my point, don't you, gentlemen? Why make a rod for our own backs?"

Slater said in a low voice, "I only know one thing with any certainty. I can't possibly face that class this afternoon, headmaster. No question of it. You'll have to get someone else."

He turned and limped out before Carter could reply. We listened to his stick tap away along the corridor. The door slammed at the far end. The voices from the playground seemed muted and far away, as if they came from another world.

"Poor fellow. Not himself. Not himself at all." Carter rubbed his hands briskly. "Right, Mr. Shaw, to you falls the post of honor."

"I see," I said. "And just what would you like me to do with it?"

It was Wally who replied. "Take the register, then straight out into the yard with them. Rounders, cricket, Swedish softball. Anything you like to keep them busy. You can let them go at three-fifteen." He turned to Carter, challenging him. "All right, head-master?"

"Excellent." Carter rubbed his hands together again, glad to have things settled. "And now, a cup of tea, I think, gentlemen."

He moved off, comfortable again in the private fantasy world of his where all was well. Wally sighed and looked around the room. "Not so good, is it?"

I nodded. "It should be a memorable afternoon."

An understatement if ever there was one.

· · ·

The rest of the staff were noticeably more cheerful when I returned to the staff room, relieved, I suppose, to know for certain that they would not be called to stand in the firing line.

The stories grew even more lurid as the lunch break drew to a close. It was clear to me that the least I could expect was to be relieved of my trousers and turned into the streets. At the other end of the scale there seemed to be a distinct possibility that I would be lynched from the lamppost outside the main gate.

When the bell for afternoon classes rang, the top class entered with the single-minded ferocity Attila the Hun and his hordes must have displayed, intent on sacking Rome.

159

I was not in the classroom to greet them, but this was a deliberate ploy on my part, for I had decided to go down fighting. To this end, I picked up the games kit from the hall cupboard en route, which meant that I was able to swing a baseball bat negligently in my right hand when I went in.

It was quite a sight. Two boys were rolling over and over in the center of the room among the desks, and the rest of the class trampled around them baying like wolves. My entrance appeared to go unnoticed. I gave them a moment, then crashed the bat down across the desk.

It had a remarkable effect. There was pin-drop silence, complete and utter stillness, every face turned toward me in astonishment. As was to be expected, it was Varley who spoke for all of them.

"Where's Mr. Slater?"

"He isn't well," I said crisply. "I'm in charge. Now sit down, all of you."

For a moment, I wasn't sure that they would, and they stood in a phalanx, glowering at me. I brought the baseball bat down again, and reluctantly, they subsided in their seats, muttering angrily.

I filled in the register, then walked out from behind the desk to confront them, hands on hips. "We're going out into the yard to play Swedish softball. You'll be released at three-fifteen, a special concession on the part of the headmaster, as this is your last day."

The voices started to rise again and I played my trump card. "Most of you will find that you'll need a letter of recommendation from the headmaster if you're to get a job. I know they're usually given to you on your final afternoon. It's been decided to change the system this year. They'll be sent on to your home address by post during the next week or so."

The implication was quite plain. Any boy who really got out of line during the afternoon could say goodbye to his letter. There was dismay on most faces, frustration and anger on some. Varley seemed to take it all rather calmly.

I told someone to bring the games kit and led the way out to the yard, feeling quite pleased with myself in a grim sort of way. I had won, they had lost, it was as simple as that.

I split them into two teams. We tossed for who batted first. It was all most amicable and incredibly orderly. Even Varley seemed happy to wait his turn halfway down the line, and it was his bovine friend, Hatch, who took the stand first.

As umpire, I stood about five yards in front of him and slightly to one side. I checked the field, then raised a finger to signal, Play. The ball was tossed, Hatch lashed out.

There was, I suppose, just a vague possibility that what happened was by design, but, to be frank, I don't think Hatch was skillful enough. In any event, he caught the ball as cleanly as anyone could hope to do and directed it at considerable speed in the general direction of my private parts.

Swedish softball is obviously a contradiction in terms when one considers the effect. I think I actually lost consciousness for a moment. When I floated to the surface again, Varley, Hatch and several other boys were clustered around me in genuine alarm.

"We'd better get him inside," Varley said.

They got an arm and a leg apiece. I think in the end there were about eight of them carrying me between them like the funeral scene in Hamlet.

The pain between my legs was unbelievable, but at least I was finished with the top class once and for all, for some other poor bastard would have to come down to the yard now and take over. It suddenly seemed to make it all worthwhile.

They must have thought me quite unhinged, for I shook with silent laughter, tears pouring down my face in spite of the agony, as they carried me inside.

· · ·

I'm not too clear as to what happened after that. When I opened my eyes, I found myself lying on the couch in Imogene's old office in the cookery room, Wally Oldroyd bending over me anxiously, Varley and Hatch peering in at the door. Poor Wally. He told me later that for one awful moment he thought they'd duffed me up in the yard when he'd seen them carrying me in.

They had sent for Imogene's successor, the girl called Harriet, who was officially in charge of all first aid. She had been supervising a netball class in the girls' yard and was dressed for the role in a sweater and a pleated tennis skirt. She had a brief conversation with Wally in the corner, then came and stood over me.

"I'd better have a look at the damage."

"Not with this lot in here you don't," I gasped.

She herded everyone outside including Wally, closed the door and shot the bolt. She returned to the couch, knelt down and proceeded to unbutton my trousers gingerly.

"Just watch it," I said in some alarm.

"I have three young brothers, Mr. Shaw," she told me calmly. "I've seen what you've got before, believe me."

All was finally revealed and she made a face. "Nasty."

I struggled into a sitting position to see for myself as she went for the first-aid kit. There was a great purple bruise the size of two half crowns across both testicles. I lay back with a groan.

"Here, have a smoke and shut up," she said as she returned with the first-aid kit and sat on the edge of the couch. "It could have been worse."

She gave me a cigarette, lit it for me, then went to work with cotton wool soaked in something or other. I pushed myself up on one elbow to watch her and was reminded suddenly of Imogene and of what had happened here in this room.

It may have been that memory which betrayed me or simply some subconscious reference to Wilma of the cigarettes and the careful hands. Suffice it to say that at one point in the proceedings, as I inhaled deeply, things began to stir.

I didn't know where on earth to put myself and tried to be jocular about it. "I'm sorry," I told her. "The beast in man rearing his ugly head as usual."

She had turned a shade pinker but otherwise seemed relatively unconcerned. "Nonsense," she said. "A perfectly understandable chemical reaction, that's all. They teach you to handle that problem in any basic nursing course, men being what they are."

She flicked sharply with her middle finger. The pain was intense, but only momentarily, and the ef

163

fect was all that could be desired, detumescence setting in rapidly.

There was a certain brutal efficiency in all this which I found intensely irritating. I wanted to get back at her in any way I could, to break through that aura of quiet breeding and superiority which surrounded her like an invisible wall.

"What are you, Methodist or Anabaptist?" I jeered. "You don't really approve of nasty things like the flesh, do you?"

"Not at all," she said calmly. "It's all right in its place, but a rather overrated pastime, I would have thought."

"Ah, I see now," I said. "Somebody hasn't been doing a very good job."

It was a rotten thing to say, and what made it worse, I'd hit the nail right on the head for she flushed deeply. I could have crawled into hiding on my belly, would gladly have done so, but there was nowhere to go.

"You can put it away now, Mr. Shaw," she said calmly in that beautifully precise upper-crust voice of hers.

She had her back turned to me as she put the first-aid kit back in the cupboard, and her shoulders started to shake. I was filled with the most terrible feelings of remorse to know I had so easily brought her to tears.

"I'm sorry," I murmured. "Truly sorry."

I turned her around gently and discovered that she was biting on her lip to contain the laughter which bubbled up spontaneously at that very moment.

"Poor Mr. Shaw," she said. "You really did look very funny."

Which certainly gave her game, set and match on that encounter.

. . .

The G.P.O., in its wisdom, altered the delivery times for our district so that the first post did not arrive until ten o'clock. During the Easter holiday this didn't matter so much, but when I was back at school it meant that I didn't know if there was any mail for me until I returned home in the evening.

When it happened, it was like being hit by lightning out of a clear blue sky. A Tuesday in April, a perfect spring evening, pale sunshine drifting in through the window, slanting across the hall table when I opened the door.

There were two letters lying there, both addressed to me. The first was some circular or other. The second was from my agent. The first paragraph conveyed the vital information that he'd had an offer for the book. An advance of two hundred pounds. Half on signature, the rest on publication, and they wanted an option on the next book.

There was more, a great deal more, but for the moment I simply couldn't take it in. Aunt Alice was in the parlor with Herr Nagel. I could hear their voices. I went into the dining room and helped myself to the sherry, then I poured another rather large one and went upstairs.

I sat at the table by the turret window and read the letter through in detail. There was the prospect of more good news in the second half, for all the signs at the New York end indicated that there was every possibility of publication over there also.

He ended on a note of caution. I must not expect too much. A great many new thrillers were published each year. To achieve average sales with this first one, both here and in the States, would be a more-than-satisfactory start.

But none of that really mattered, and I sat there at the turret window savoring the golden moment, my own private celebration. People who knew about such things actually wanted my work. Were prepared to pay for it. I was a writer, a professional in every sense of the word at last, and nothing would ever, could ever, be the same again.

• • •

I went down to the parlor to break the news to Aunt Alice. To be honest, it fell a bit flat, and not because she wasn't interested. It was just that she seemed to take it in such an irritatingly offhand way. It was inevitable. She had always known it would happen because one of the most important aspects in my map was Sun trine Jupiter. She appealed to Herr Nagel for confirmation on this point. With his usual benign smile he supplied further technical details which were above me. I made my excuses and fled.

Jake was still in London, so once again there was no one to tell. For a moment I had one of those depression *déjà vu* feelings of having been here before, but not for long. I had a bath, changed into my best suit, got five pounds from my mad-money tin and went out into the golden evening.

• • •

Everything seemed different, clearer, sharper, as if suddenly I was possessed of some extra vision. I have seldom felt happier than I did on the top deck of the tram that evening as we rattled along the track across the playing fields, creaking and groaning like a ship under sail.

Everything was the same, yet not the same. Changed, changed completely, people and things, because *I* had changed. It was a feeling I simply couldn't shake off. Not then on the top deck of the tram, or later in the lounge bar of The Tall Man. I had suddenly become some sort of outsider, a man on the periphery of things, watching the antics of more ordinary mortals with a kind of detached curiosity.

As I say, the feelings simply wouldn't go away. Some sort of reaction, I suppose, and later at the Trocadero, I felt even more detached than ever. Who was I? What was I doing here? The saxophones droned "Night and Day," the dancers circled in a blue mist, locked in each other's arms. For some reason I felt quite sad and cut off from all human contact.

A moment later the lights went up and the bandleader announced a ladies' choice. I stayed where I was, leaning against a pillar by the bandstand in a brown study, aware of the girl in the blue silk dress walking toward me. Aware, yet not aware . . . When she asked me to dance I moved toward the floor automatically. It was only as she started to laugh when I took her in my arms that I realized it was Harriet.

"What's wrong with you, for heaven's sake?" she demanded. "You look like death."

We had reached the other end of the floor, and on impulse I took her by the hand and pulled her upstairs to the balcony. When I sat her at a table by the rail she looked thoroughly bewildered. I took the letter from my inside pocket and dropped it on the table.

"Read that," I commanded. "I'll get you a coffee."

When I returned, she looked up at me wide-eyed. "But this is marvelous, Oliver. I never realized."

I sat down, shaking like a leaf, and she leaned across the table, concern on her face, and put a hand on mine. "Are you all right?"

"I had to get a reaction from someone," I said. "Now I can really believe it. Can you understand that?"

"Of course."

Her hand stayed in mine, and I was aware, and not for the first time, of what a very great comfort a woman can be. "Someone's opened a restaurant in an old house near the park," I said. "They tell me it's very good. Italian food, a three-piece band, the works, and I've got five pounds burning a hole in my pocket. What do you say?"

She smiled delightfully and stood up. "Give me two minutes to get my coat and I'll be right with you."

• • •

It was really quite an evening, for the place exceeded my wildest expectations. Food restrictions in restaurants had not been lifted very long, but it all seemed more than adequate to me. We had a Dover sole apiece, some sort of pasta and a full bottle of Pouilly Fuissé, so cold that it seemed to burn its way down.

The trio, I suspect, wasn't up to much in reality. A woman pianist and two men, one on the drums and another who played guitar and sang.

We danced a great deal, I remember that, for the place wasn't particularly busy and we had the tiny floor to ourselves. What does come back to me with absolute clarity was leaving at eleven and finding that it was pouring outside which for some reason seemed absolutely right.

We were both pretty tight by then, which was only to be expected, and Harriet seemed like another person as she ran ahead of me in the rain, tight-roping along the pavement edge, laughing constantly.

The streets were quite deserted, particularly the quiet area of old Victorian houses where she lived on the far side of the park. I had never felt so alive, so conscious of the infinite possibilities of life.

At one point we paused at the end of an old stone-walled ginnel to shelter while I attempted to light a cigarette. There was a gas lamp in a bracket above our heads, rain drifting down through it in a silver mist. Harriet stood underneath, her face upturned in a kind of ecstasy.

"Isn't life marvelous, Oliver?"

Strange, but I can still hear that voice echoing through the years. For a moment she reminded me of Imogene, and I moved close, taking her in my arms, but when I attempted to kiss her, she stiffened, then seemed to shrink away.

"We'd better move on."

Which we did, although there was a constraint between us now which seemed unnecessary and was certainly a great pity.

The house surprised me. A Gothic brick palace in an enormous garden converted into eight flats, she informed me when we reached the gate. Hers was on the ground floor, and we followed a path to the side which eventually led to a flagged terrace with a balustrade.

"I usually go in this way." She took a key from her handbag and unlocked one of the French windows. "It's much more convenient."

"It must be nice in the summer," I said.

"If you'd like to come in, I could make some coffee." I hesitated, that constraint still between us, and she reached up and kissed me briefly on the cheek. "Please, Oliver, I really do make rather excellent coffee."

• • •

Which was a simple statement of fact—I acknowledged that much to myself as we sat later by the open window in the darkness, a small table between us.

I had to say something so I tried apologizing. "I'm sorry," I said.

"What for?"

"Some of the things I said to you that day in your office were unforgivable."

"But you were right," she said simply. "Absolutely."

There was a slight pause, and then she started to talk about it. Of being seventeen in 1945, the last summer of the war, and the cousin who had conva-

lesced with her family for three months. A second
lieutenant of infantry with a slight leg wound. The
romantic figure who could do no wrong, the only
trouble being that whatever he had done, he had
not done very well . . .

And she was worth more than that. I sat there in
the darkness when she had finished talking, remembering, for a rather obvious reason, Helen. Remembering her kindness, her gentleness in a very similar
situation.

I don't know why, but I suddenly felt that I owed
it to her to do something. That there was a debt here
that needed repaying in the only way I knew how.

I stood up and reached for Harriet's hand. "Come
on," I said gently. "Let's go to bed."

For a moment I thought she might say no, suspect,
even now, that it was one of those knife-edge deci-
sions on which so much of life seems to depend,
and then she stood up, came into my arms and
kissed me.

"All right, Oliver, give me five minutes."

I lit a cigarette, had another coffee, sitting there
by the open window, not really thinking about anything in particular, but somehow terribly aware of
my existence. Of being a part of the night, of the
spring rain, the smell of damp earth. It was as if I
had never been truly conscious of myself before.

She called my name so softly that I hardly heard
her, and when I went into the other room, she was
already in bed with the light out. I undressed and
got in beside her. When I took her in my arms she
started to tremble as I had trembled earlier in the
evening, and I gentled her, stroking her hair.

Gradually the trembling stopped and she moved

closer. For the first time in such a situation I was conscious that I wanted nothing for myself. That the only important person here this night was she. Time ceased to have any relevance at all. I only know that when I finally took her she was absolutely ready. She gasped my name once, the only word she had spoken during the entire business. To be frank, I was rather proud of myself as I lay beside her, her head pillowed on my shoulder, listening to the rain drumming against the window.

"Was it all right?" I asked her softly after a minute or so.

She turned and kissed me in the hollow between neck and shoulder, and her voice, when she spoke, was rather muffled. "I don't love you, you do understand that?"

"Of course."

She sighed heavily. "Having made that point quite clear, I really would be greatly obliged, Oliver, if you'd do it again."

· · ·

The second letter from my agent arrived just over a week later and I found it, as with the other, waiting for me on the hall table when I got home from school.

It was confirmation of the American offer, an advance of one thousand dollars, which at the current rate of exchange was worth approximately three hundred and fifty pounds. This time there was someone to tell, as Jake was due home on the London train that very afternoon.

He must have seen me coming through the garden for he appeared at the top of the fire escape as

I ran across the yard. "Now then, old sport," he called cheerfully.

He knew about the original offer for the book, as I had written to him about it, and I pushed the present letter into his hand and followed him into the room, almost panting with excitement.

He looked up after reading it, genuinely pleased. "Marvelous, Oliver, bloody marvelous, and no more than you deserve."

I sprawled in a chair and waited as he poured whiskey into a couple of glasses and brought them over. "And now my news," he said as he gave me my drink.

"Good God!" I said, thunderstruck. "You've passed your exams."

"I'm afraid so." He grinned delightedly and raised his glass. "To us, old sport, the both of us, and let the good times roll."

He dropped into the opposite chair. "Just think, Oliver. Now I can get down to my writing with a clear conscience. Don't want to be a bloody solicitor all my life."

"Of course you can," I said.

It was another of those moments of perfection in life when all things seem possible and we savored it for a moment; then Jake jumped to his feet, rubbing his hands together.

"This calls for a celebration. We'll start at The Tall Man and work our way to town, pub by pub, and finish the evening at Murphy's."

As it happened, I had a date with Harriet, having promised to take her to the theater. I had just left her for we had come home from school together. Since that first memorable evening our affair had ripened in a very satisfactory way. In fact, I'd been in the habit of sleeping at her place most nights.

"We'll take her with us," Jake said when I explained.

I couldn't really see Harriet in Murphy's, that was the thing, and I said so, but Jake wouldn't take no for an answer.

"Leave her to me, old sport, I'll handle her. We'll have one hell of an evening, I promise you. She'll love it."

Even now, in spite of the intervening years, my bowels contract at the thought of it.

• • •

Persuade her he did indeed, for when the Irishman in him took over, Jake could charm the birds off the trees. In any case, Harriet took to him immediately, and Jake, delighted, as he informed me at one point, to find that for once I had found myself a lady, put himself out to please.

The pub crawl he had intended was severely curtailed; we only went into the better bars and drank shorts instead of beer. It was all very civilized, and any idea of ending the evening at Murphy's had obviously vanished from his mind. The trouble was that at one point in the proceedings he mentioned the place to Harriet who immediately declared that she'd like to see for herself what it was like.

Which was enough for Jake, who by that time had decided she should be denied nothing. I was pretty well floating by then, not having his head for liquor, and was in no condition to argue.

I tried, however, but he waved me down. "One

drink, old sport, that's all, just to show her how the other half live, and then we'll go, I promise you."

And that was very much that, for he whistled up a cab from the City Square rank and a moment later we were away.

. . .

Murphy's was an alehouse rather than a pub, a tall, decaying pile of rotting brick that stood like a sore thumb in the middle of a bombsite by the river which had been cleared for new housing. There was music on the night air, voices raised in song, a considerable amount of laughter, and when we ventured in, the bar was packed, for it was near to closing time.

On my own I wouldn't have lasted five minutes in there, as this was an Irish boozer and outsiders, meaning the bloody English, weren't welcome. Jake was Irish enough for any man in spite of his Yorkshire upbringing and well known in the district.

He was warmly greeted by several rough-looking individuals and by the landlord himself, a one-eyed giant called Sean Murphy, with a tangled gray beard and broken teeth, an ex-heavyweight boxer who always reminded me uncomfortably of the great Victor McLaglen in one of those roles where he looks ready to clear the bar on his own at any moment.

Indeed, most of the gentlemen there that night bore a resemblance to Victor McLaglen, at least in my befuddled mind. I accepted the pint of Guinness someone thrust into my hand and sank into a corner seat. Harriet loved it, every awful minute, and the Irish, ever gentlemen where women are concerned, whoever else gets the back of their hand, made much of her.

I remember her sitting on the bar at one point while someone serenaded her with "Mother Machree" to an accordion accompaniment. Then a handsome young man with a face like the devil himself beneath his battered cloth cap sang "The Lark in the Clear Air" in Irish in a tenor voice that would not have disgraced the Albert Hall, a voice of such haunting beauty that several patrons at the bar cried openly.

I very obviously slept after that, God knows for how long, but I came back to life to find the bar empty except for Murphy himself, who was playing a melodeon, Harriet on a stool, still looking as fresh as a daisy, and Jake, who seemed to be executing some kind of Irish jig on the bar itself.

Murphy was singing at the top of his voice, a dreadful song which apparently concerned itself with the ambush of a group of Black-and-Tans at some place called Macroom.

I glanced at my watch and saw that it was just past midnight. I got to my feet, Jake waved to me, and at the same moment there was a thunderous knocking on the door.

"Police!" a voice called. "Open up!"

Murphy was round the bar in a second, an apron in his hand, which he shoved at Harriet. "Get that on and behind the bar quick, and start washing glasses."

"What about us?" Jake whispered.

"Upstairs to bed with you and be quiet."

It seemed a sensible enough idea for I knew he rented beds by the night to itinerant Irish laborers.

Jake grabbed me by the arm and shoved me out into the passage as Murphy moved to the door grumbling.

"Would ye hold on to your patience for a while?" we heard him call as we reached the landing.

The police were inside a moment later, boots pounding, and Jake opened the nearest door and shoved me inside. There was a double bed, I remember that quite distinctly. I remember also climbing between the sheets fully clothed for there was hardly time to undress.

A moment later the door opened and a man appeared in a cloth cap, donkey jacket and dungarees, one of Murphy's single-night tenants, as it transpired later, who had been having some supper in the kitchen. He was obviously very drunk. He lifted the blankets and got in on the other side of Jake, fully clothed, cloth cap and all.

"Move over and give a fella a bit of room here," he grumbled.

A split second later the door was flung open, and a large police sergeant entered followed by two constables of equal dimensions. He stood looking down at us, hands on hips.

"What have we got here, the babes in the woods?" he demanded and pulled the blankets to one side. "Do you usually go to bed with your shoes on?"

"Only when my feet are cold," Jake said.

• • •

By some miracle, the ploy with Harriet worked, and she was allowed to depart, vanishing instantly into the night. Murphy, Jake, myself and the unfortunate laborer who had got into bed with us were nothing like as lucky, for English law seems to consider drinking after hours roughly on the same level as rape, assault with a deadly weapon and armed robbery.

They sent for a Black Maria. Within half an hour, we were being booked into the local Bridewell by a granite-faced desk sergeant who looked as if he'd seen everything there ever was to see.

It was an interesting experience, especially the moment when he asked my profession and I had to answer "Schoolmaster." The look on his face was enough, and my heart sank like a stone.

I don't know whether the drink had finally got to Jake, or what, but he became more than a little awkward when his turn came, adopting the kind of Abbey Theatre accent the English fondly imagine to be typical of the Irish, referring to the sergeant as "Yer Honor," which that worthy did not appreciate at all.

"Pull yourself together, O'Reilly," he snapped at one point. "This kind of conduct isn't going to get you anywhere. Now what's your profession?"

"Ah, that's aisy, Yer Honor," Jake told him. "Solicitor's clerk, wit, bon viveur, sportsman, raconteur, soldier of the Irish Republican Army and all-round good egg."

Our fate was sealed, and we were remanded together to face the worst that the bench had to offer on the following morning.

• • •

I passed the night in a drunken stupor, which was still with me when we were led into court at ten-thirty. I noticed Harriet sitting by the door. As I found out later, she'd simply taken the morning off from school. Jake waved to her and was sharply brought to order by the clerk, who proceeded to read out the charges.

For some reason, Jake had been listed as "laborer," possibly because the sergeant had been unable to take the choice he had offered him seriously, or, more possibly, because that seemed the right sort of job for someone with a name like O'Reilly. However, I was still listed as "schoolmaster," there was no avoiding that.

The magistrate, an aging, world-weary gentleman who had listened to the police sergeant's stolid account of the whole affair with obvious distaste, turned his wrath, at the end of the account, particularly in my direction.

"These other poor wretches have acted in a manner which can only be described as typical of their type, but you, Shaw—" here he glowered at me over the tops of his spectacles—"a man of education. A schoolmaster. For you there can be no excuse. Indeed I can only hope that your disgraceful conduct is brought to the attention of the proper authorities."

In the face of such virulence I found it difficult to believe that I was only being charged with drinking on licensed premises after hours. Murphy, Jake and the laborer were fined two pounds each. I was charged a fiver. So much for justice.

We were free within the hour, Jake having been allowed to phone a colleague who soon appeared with the necessary funds. Harriet was waiting at the top of the Town Hall steps when we went out into the pale morning sunshine.

She rushed to my side, concern on her face, and took my arm. "I'm sorry, Oliver, honestly I am."

"That's all right," I told her. "It wasn't your fault."

"But it was," she replied instantly. "After all, I did insist on visiting the wretched place. You made it quite clear you thought it wasn't such a good idea from the beginning, but Jake wouldn't listen."

She glared accusingly at Jake, who made himself scarce at once and left us to it.

"Does Carter know?" I asked.

She shook her head. "Not yet."

"He will," I said. "You can bet your sweet life on that."

*   *   *

It was on page two of the local paper that evening. The inside page, perhaps, but it didn't really matter, for they had done me proud with a nice black headline all to myself. *Local teacher appears before bench.* There was a lot more in smaller print, including the magistrate's comments.

The following morning Carter called me out of my classroom and spoke to me in the corridor. "I've had a phone call from the office about you, Shaw," he said coldly. "You're to call in after school. Mr. Crosby wants to see you. Four-thirty sharp."

"All right," I said.

He started to turn away, then suddenly rounded on me, quivering with indignation. "It really is quite disgraceful. I don't know how you can show your face."

I told him where to go in very succinct Anglo-Saxon, advancing toward him at the same moment. It worked splendidly, for the cigarette fell from his lips as his mouth gaped in alarm, and he was off like a shot.

. . .

When I was shown into Crosby's office that evening I found Dawson with him. They remained seated behind the desk, frowning on me sternly. The atmosphere was nothing like as cordial as it had been on that first occasion.

"I'll make it easy for you," I said. "You can have my resignation."

"I'd like to remind you that the contract you signed runs till the end of this term, Shaw," Crosby said sharply.

"Look, let's get this over with," I said. "What am I here for?"

"It's a question of standards, Shaw," Dawson said earnestly. "Of common decency. I mean to say, you've behaved disgracefully, you must see that."

"We've the morals of the children of this city to think of," Crosby put in.

It really was too ludicrous for words when one considered they were willing to employ a man like Carter. "One of our most able headmasters" was how Crosby had referred to him. But by then I'd had enough of this farce. Of stupid, petty little men who were only interested in expressing their authority.

"Look, do you want my resignation or not?" I demanded.

"At the end of the term," Crosby said.

"As laid down in your contract," Dawson added. "Needless to say, you've failed your probationary year."

"Gentlemen, I thank you."

I louted low, gave them a very stiff two fingers each and walked out.

. . .

I had some tea at a Lyons café and went to the cinema. *Kiss Tomorrow Goodbye* with James Cagney at one point knocking the merry hell out of a man who bore a remarkable resemblance to Dawson, which cheered me considerably. I enjoyed it all immensely. When I left at about nine o'clock I found it was raining again.

I walked all the way home full of energy and enormously cheerful in spite of what had happened. A few more weeks and Khyber Street would be behind me, and what could be bad about that?

When I let myself in at the front door there was another letter waiting for me from my agent, which I could tell at a glance because he'd taken to using envelopes with his name and address printed on the flap.

My heart started to beat a little faster; a finger touched me coldly in the pit of the stomach, a premonition of disaster. Something had gone wrong, I knew it. I sat down, opened the letter carefully and discovered that he'd had an offer for the film rights to the book.

. . .

I sat there for a long, long moment, quite stunned, then reread the letter slowly to make sure I hadn't made any mistake. But I was right the first time. Two hundred pounds for a year's option against an eventual price of two thousand if the film was ever made.

I did a quick sum in my head. British and American book rights and now this, giving me a grand total of seven hundred and fifty pounds in advances. *About double my annual salary as a teacher at Khyber Street.*

I think I did the run through the garden to Jake's in record time. There was a light at his window. I paused at the top of the fire escape to peer inside and found him on the couch with his pretty war widow, Mrs. Tarrant.

Which left Harriet, so I buttoned up my trench coat and set off in the rain, taking the shortcut through the park. Dear Harriet, she'd really come to mean a great deal to me during the past couple of weeks. I suppose the plain truth was that she had everything. As someone once said, brains, good looks and a whore in bed.

I moved a little more quickly, just thinking about her, but when I reached the house and went up the drive there was no light in her window. I climbed to the terrace and rapped on one of the panes.

After a while, a lamp was switched on in her bedroom and the window was raised a little. "Who is it?" she called.

"Oliver." I moved to the window. "Let me in. I've got some wonderful news."

"Oliver?" She sounded half asleep. "What time is it?"

I pushed the letter into her hand. "Go on, read that. Guaranteed to bring you wide awake."

And it did. She moved to the lamp beside the bed, her limbs showing through the silk nightgown enticingly, and was back in a moment.

"Oh, Oliver, how wonderful. I'm so happy for you."

She gave me the letter, leaned out the window and kissed me. I stood there in the rain, holding her lightly, inhaling the fragrance of her hair, and suddenly knew what I wanted to do—what was the right thing to do.

"Marry me, Harriet," I said. "I can afford a wife now."

She drew back. "Marry you?"

I was piqued at the tone of her voice and showed it, and she smiled gently with genuine concern. "Look, Oliver, you're lovely, you really are, and you've certainly been very good for me in the more basic areas of life, but there's got to be more than that, hasn't there?" She shrugged. "Anyway, I had news, too. I'm going to Canada at the end of the term. My father's taking over as managing director of a new subsidiary in Toronto, and I've promised to go with him."

I said lamely, "Well, that's that."

She said "You can come in. A farewell party, if you like."

But that was no good. No good at all. "No, thanks," I said. "I'd better be getting back before I start the dogs howling."

She sighed. "Dear Oliver, I owe you such a lot. I really do." She kissed me gently, leaning out over the sill, then closed the window, and I was alone.

• • •

Jake and I, walking through the city center after midnight from some dance or other, had been in the habit of calling in at the central railway station because there was an all-night café where you could get tea or coffee and sandwiches. The station was a great Victorian barn of a place, cold and with the taste of steam on the air, deserted at that time of night, platforms disappearing into the shadows. It always filled me with a desperate unease.

I wrote a poem about it which I found in an old notebook years later and gave to a character in one of my later novels. It had to do with life sometimes being like getting on the wrong train and not being able to get off. *No way of getting back to where you started,* that was the line.

That night, standing there in the rain, I should have been happy, yet was filled with that same irrational sense of unease, the railway feeling all over again. Rather like setting off on the wrong journey. It was as if on one of those long walks home in the rain on a Saturday night after a dance I'd taken the first on the right when I should have taken the second on the left. It was a feeling that haunted me for years and still does.

But not then, standing there outside Harriet's window. It was nonsense—had to be. I pushed the thought firmly away, walked down the path and turned along the road. The rain rushed through the trees and I paused under a lamp and realized I was still clutching the letter from my agent.

They never did film that book, and all I received was the option money. But there were others over the years that followed, many of them, and there I still stand, caught in that timeless moment in the lamplight, the ink on the envelope beginning to run in the rain. No matter. Nothing could take the actuality of that letter away, then or now.

There had to be something more—Harriet had said that, and she was right. I think it happened then, as Jake had said it might from the beginning, with a sudden rush, a kind of release as if a tremendous energy locked up inside me had now broken free.

There *was* something more, waiting for me at the end of the street around the corner, and I was free to find it. Really free. A hell of a year in more ways than one but it had been worth it.

I put the letter in my pocket and walked home through the rain, content.

ABOUT THE AUTHOR

Born in England, Jack Higgins was raised in Belfast by his mother's Irish family. She remarried when he was eleven, and he moved to England, to Leeds, in Yorkshire, to live with her and his stepfather. Conscripted into the army at eighteen he joined the Household Cavalry Training Regiment at Windsor, then served as an NCO with the Royal Horse Guards on the East German border and in Berlin during the Cold War. Demobilized in September 1949, he returned to Leeds, where *Memoirs of a Dance-Hall Romeo* takes up his story.